Chased

Love like Yours, Book #4

NICOLE S. GOODIN

Chased
Love like Yours Series – Book #4
Published by Nicole S. Goodin

ISBN: 978-0-473-40443-7

Chased
First published July 2017
Cover design by Nicole Goodin
Images purchased from Deposit Photos
Edited by Spell Bound

For Iain.

Chased is book #4 in the Love like Yours Series.

A lot of people had a real soft spot for poor Colt, and they weren't too happy when he got his heart broken in Hunted, I hope this helps!

"Settle your heart, child, your time will come. One of these days you will meet eyes with someone who makes you feel so at home in the world you will think to yourself, ah, there you are."
- Beau Taplin

Prologue

Colt

I reached blindly for my ringing phone.

Jesus... make it stop.

The shrill ringtone was making my brain feel like it was going to explode out of my skull.

I reached around again and knocked over a glass of water; it fell from the table and smashed onto the ground.

Fuck.

I was way too hungover for this shit... but whoever the bastard on the other end of the line was, they weren't giving up.

Where the fuck is that phone?

I lifted my head from the pillow and groaned, regretting the movement instantly.

That extra round of tequila shots was not my finest decision.

I rolled over and spotted the source of all the noise in the middle of the floor, next to my gigantic pile of dirty laundry.

I groaned again. This room needed cleaning something chronic.

When did I become such a slob?

I sat up slowly and tried to settle my pounding head. I swung my legs out of the bed and reached for the phone, only then realizing I was butt naked.

I am NEVER drinking again.

"Hello?" I answered with a grumble, not even bothering to check the screen to see who was calling.

"What's up your ass?" Harrison, my oldest brother, chuckled. "You still drunk or something?"

Bastard.

Harrison never called me this early; so my guess was someone at the club had told him I'd been hitting the bottle again.

"You know me..." I deadpanned, feeling too close to death to even bother giving him a real response.

He wasn't exactly wrong anyway. This was becoming somewhat of a habit for me lately. When the club closed for the night, I sat around with the staff getting shit-faced.

"You sober enough for a business chat?"

I glanced at my clock; it was eight in the morning on a Sunday.

What the hell?

"It's Sunday morning, man, what do you want that couldn't wait until to-morrow?" I crawled back into bed, feeling sicker than I could ever remember feeling.

"Yeah... sorry," he replied, not sounding in the least bit sorry at all. "But I'm on limited time. Safe and Sound needs a venue for a black tie fundraiser. We'd booked a ballroom down town, but they've cancelled because of water dam-age... had a flood or some shit."

Jesus.

"And you want the club," I stated.

"You got it in one," he replied.

"When?" I asked.

"Friday," he answered.

Friday? Is he joking?

"As in Friday, in 5 days' time, Friday?" I asked, certain that I must have been mistaken.

Surely he's not that unreasonable...

"Yeah... it's short notice I know..."

I rubbed my temples – this extra stress was not helping the situation going on inside my head at all.

"Can't you postpone?" I all but begged.

"No can do, little bro, tickets are sold, the entertainment is flying in the day before... it's definitely happening Friday."

"You're not actually asking me are you?" I attempted to roll my eyes and re-gretted it instantly.

"Not really," he stated. "Let's say I'm *informing* you."

I knew I couldn't say no to him. He owned as much of the club as I did.

"Fine." I sighed. "But the club stays open. You can have the V.I.P. floor and your guests can use the west entrance. You bring caterers. I'll get extra security."

Now just leave me the hell alone.

I could almost feel his elation at having got his way. "I knew I could count on you. Quinn will get hold of you to get the place decorated later in the week."

Shit.

Quinn...

The state I was in right now, I couldn't even imagine having to deal with my ex-girlfriend – my brother's current. Her choosing him still stung like a bitch, and that was from the comfort of my own home, not up close and personal.

"Yeah, yeah. I gotta go," I mumbled.

"Thanks, I do appreciate it, Col—"

I hung up before he could finish his sentence.

Fuck.

Quinn.

I'll have to talk to her... I'll have to be around her and Harrison together...

I bolted for the bathroom and threw up loudly into the toilet.

"Eye contact and a heartbeat. That's how it began."
- Author unknown

1. Lexie

"This place is beautiful, Q." I sighed as I looked out the window of Harrison's truck. "I can see why you love it here."

Harrison and Quinn had picked me up from the airport, and I had been beyond excited to see her. I couldn't wait to see Ellerslie too; she was at some toddler music class with Stella and was going to bring her around to Harrison's place after.

I smiled at the thought.

She's all about being a mom now.

"You should see it covered in snow," Quinn replied, her voice all dreamy sounding.

I grinned at her and Harrison, holding hands over the center console. They looked incredibly happy together. I knew they'd had some problems over the past few months, but whatever those problems were, they seemed to be nothing but ancient history now.

"So tell me about tomorrow night," I instructed, excitement coursing through my body.

I was going to be singing at their fundraiser event tomorrow night. Quinn and Harrison, along with Ellerslie, Lawson, Logan, Reeve and his girlfriend, Lisa, had started a foundation called 'Safe and Sound'. They used it to help victims who hadn't been given justice inside the court room. They were hosting a black tie event, and I was the entertainment.

I loved singing, dancing too. Even though I got to perform nearly every day I still got a total thrill out of it every single time I got up on a stage in front of a crowd.

My friends all thought I was mad for working as much as I did, but they didn't get it. Singing didn't feel like work to me. It was my passion, and I was grateful each and every time people took the time to listen to me perform. That, and the fact that I got to cruise around on a luxury ship... there were zero complaints from me about how I spent my time.

"We had a last-minute venue change," Quinn replied, before peeking at Harrison out the corner of her eye, a sheepish look on her face. "And Colt has agreed to let us have it at the club that he, Harrison and their other brother, Mitch, own."

She added the bit about Colt in a rush, like she didn't really want to be talking about him, but decided not mentioning him would be just as awkward.

I saw the corner of Harrison's mouth twitch in amusement – he'd obviously noticed her reaction too.

I tried to hold back a giggle but it slipped out anyway.

Harrison chuckled loudly and squeezed Quinn's hand. "You can say his name, Skippy." He laughed again. "I'm not that unreasonable, am I?"

Quinn laughed. "Yeah that was weird. I don't know why I did that, sorry."

"So what's this club like?" I asked.

"It's the best club this city's got," Harrison bragged as he peeked at me in the rearview mirror. "It's where all the kids are hanging out." He chuckled.

I saw Quinn roll her eyes at him.

"We've got the whole V.I.P. floor; we'll have a stage set up for you and that band you recommended," Quinn told me.

She had it all figured out.

"Sounds perfect. I've got a song list here if you want to check it."

She shook her head. "That's all good. I trust ya, Lex." She turned around and winked at me. "So, tell me all about what's been happening on the ship."

***

I squeezed El tight when we reached the front door. I'd loved every minute of catching up with her and Lawson, and I'd been instantly smitten with Stella.

"I can't wait for tomorrow night. After my set we'll have a few drinks... and a few dances." I nudged her elbow with mine.

"I bet we will." El giggled.

"It'll be just like old times." Lawson's eyes sparkled as he looked down at his wife.

"Had a few good nights at 'The L', huh?" I asked him with a grin.

"You wouldn't believe," he murmured back to me, still not taking his eyes off Ellerslie.

That's a whole lot of heat...

"And you, Stella girl..." I crouched down to her level. "You have the best time with uncle Rome."

Stella grinned at me.

"You keep him busy, alright?"

She nodded her head.

"Slap me some skin, baby girl." I held up my hand for a high five, and she tapped her tiny hand against it daintily.

"Bye, Wexie." She wrapped her arms around my neck and squeezed me tight.

"See you soon, beautiful," I whispered into her blonde hair.

Lawson hoisted Stella up onto his shoulders, and she shrieked with glee.

The three of them stepped outside and started down the front steps towards Lawson's truck.

They really are the perfect little family.

"See you tomorrow," I called after them.

"See ya, Lex." El waved.

"See ya, Wex," Stella mimicked.

I giggled as I shut the door. That little girl was the cutest thing I'd ever seen.

***

"Do you want me to help with anything today?" I asked Quinn as I loaded the dishwasher.

The fundraiser event was tonight, and I had no idea how much work Quinn still had to get done before then.

Harrison had left for the office already. He had to meet a client this morning and I'd heard him tell Q that he'd probably be able to be at the club at about three this afternoon.

"I have to go into work and get Macie set up for the rest of the day, and then I'll head down to start on the decorations. The company is waving the hire fee, but I have to set everything up myself," she replied with a nervous expression.

"I'll help," I offered. "What time do you need me?"

She smiled gratefully. "They're not arriving until midday. Could you meet me there about half twelve?"

I nodded. "Can you leave me the number for a cab?"

"It's on the board by the phone." She pointed as she sat her empty coffee cup in the sink.

"Perfect. I need to get a dress for tonight, so I can sort that out this morning, then I'm all yours."

"Thank you! You are a lifesaver, Lexie Chase." Quinn grabbed her bag and headed for the door. "Call me if you need me!" she yelled out before shutting the door behind her.

***

"Are you fucking kidding me?" I heard Quinn screech.

Oh shit.

At least that explains why she didn't answer the phone.

I'd spent my morning shopping before taking a cab over to the club. I'd arrived just after half past, but I had no idea where to go once I was there. I'd tried to call Quinn three times, but it was engaged. One of the waitresses had eventually arrived and shown me where I needed to go.

"You realize it's *tonight*, right?" she yelled.

Crap...

That didn't sound good.

I reached the top of the landing and Quinn came into view. She had her phone to her ear as she paced the room, and she looked like she wanted to rip someone's head off.

She caught sight of me as she spun around and shot me a grateful smile.

I waved and stayed where I was. An angry Quinn wasn't something I wanted to get involved with.

"I've fucking had it with you," she announced. "You can take your half-hearted apology and shove it up your ass!" She pulled the phone away from her ear and hung up.

I grimaced. That was definitely not good.

"Jesus, Quinn, what the hell are you yelling about?" a male voice spoke before I could.

Quinn spun around with a murderous look in her eye, and I didn't envy whoever it was that had just poked the beast.

Surprisingly though, she didn't tear strips off whoever had spoken. Instead, she took a deep, calming breath and muttered something to herself. I saw a guy walking towards her, he looked older than me, but still young. He had blond hair, with a slim build and was slightly taller than Quinn.

This guy has to be Colt.

I shook my head in amusement. Quinn had managed to get herself into quite the predicament here.

"The goddamn band cancelled," she told him by way of an excuse for her outburst.

Crap.

She looked back over to me. "I'm so sorry, Lex."

The guy, who I was going to assume was Colt until I was told otherwise, noticed me for the first time. His eyes gave me a lazy head to toe; appraising my tight black jeans, fitted white top and black Nikes. My long, dark hair was loose down my back and I had thrown a small amount of makeup on.

I made my way over to the two of them and reached my hand out to him. "Hey, I'm Lexie."

He took my hand and regarded me curiously. "Colt," he replied.

I was right.

I stared hard at him, trying to figure out the gorgeous man in front of me – there was no point in denying he was gorgeous. His eyes were a mix of hazel and gold, and were framed with thick lashes. His body looked tight and toned underneath his fitted t-shirt.

I can see the family resemblance.

He looked a lot like his brother, but there was something in his eyes. He looked... *lost*... like he didn't really belong here... or maybe it was that he simply didn't *want* to be here.

Maybe he's not over Quinn.

He still hadn't released my hand.

I tugged on it slightly and he looked down and frowned. "Sorry," he muttered, letting go of me.

I felt unnerved for some reason; I couldn't put my finger on what it was exactly that was causing the sensation.

The obvious awkwardness between Colt and Q maybe?

Whatever it was, it had me feeling incredibly off balance.

I looked back at Quinn. "Don't worry about the band. It's no biggie. I can sing acapella, or we can use backing tracks," I suggested.

"Wait, *you're* the singer?" Colt asked in disbelief before Quinn could reply.

I narrowed my eyes at him. "Why do you sound so surprised?" I demanded, my voice showing just how unappreciated his tone was.

His shocked expression softened at my obvious annoyance. "No... it's just because I heard you had a huge voice. And you're so tiny. I just..." He trailed off. "Never mind." He shook his head, presumably at his own stupidity.

I ignored him.

"Honestly, Q, it'll be fine. I don't need a band. Even just a guitarist would have been helpful, but we'll manage."

It'll be fine. This is what I do.

2. Colt

"I'll do it," I found myself saying before I'd even thought it through.

I was still looking at the petite, beautiful, little woman in front of me.

Lexie.

For some reason I just felt the need to make it up to her, after I'd clearly offended her with my last comment.

Idiot.

"Wait..." Quinn looked back and forth between the two of us. "You'll do what?"

"Play the guitar for her," I clarified, pointing at Lexie.

"*You* play?" Quinn asked, shock evident in her voice. "Since when?" she demanded.

I looked back at her and smirked. "Since I was about six years old."

Guess she never knew me that well after all.

Her mouth made an 'o' shape. "Are you sure? I can ask Lawson, he plays pretty well."

"Nah, it's cool. I'll do it. Lawson can enjoy his night off."

I glanced at both the women in front of me, Quinn looked surprised, and Lexie looked curious. They also both looked incredibly grateful.

Maybe even a little impressed.

I wasn't sure why I gave a shit about impressing either of them, but I realized that I did.

Old habits die hard I guess.

"Well alright then," Quinn agreed. "Ah... thanks, Colt..."

The air between us was tense and awkward.

Her phone rang again and she groaned. "Excuse me." She shot Lexie an apologetic glance before taking her call.

I turned to Lexie. "So... have you got a song list planned out?"

She nodded enthusiastically. "I sure do." She rummaged through the bag she had slung over her shoulder.

I couldn't help but notice how pretty she was as I watched her – I was a man after all, and beauty like that was pretty hard to miss.

She grinned triumphantly as she found what she was looking for. "Here." She passed me a sheet of paper.

I quickly scanned the list.

Adele, Ed Sheeran, Sam Hunt, Zara Larsson, John Legend...

Good songs.

"You sure know how to pick them," I told her with a smile.

"Ah... thanks?" she said it like a question.

I sat down at one of the nearby tables and gestured for her to do the same.

"Did you have any arrangements in mind?" I asked.

"I was basically going to stick to the originals," she replied as she sat down next to me.

"We might have to go unplugged for a few..." I tapped my pen on the table, getting a feel for the beat of a few of the songs.

"These ones..." She leaned over and pointed to a few on the list. "They'll be perfect for a more acoustic performance."

Her arm brushed mine as she reached for the sheet of paper, and my skin prickled. She was right in close, and I couldn't help but breathe in the scent of her shampoo. Her hair smelled like a bunch of flowers.

"We could add in more Ed...? He really lends himself to that style," she suggested.

"Mm hmm." I nodded, still distracted by the smell of her.

She turned her head and looked up at me with bright eyes. "What do you think about toning the whole thing down? Ballads... folk... all acoustic?"

I swallowed deeply and nodded my head, one short, jerky bob. "Yeah, that sounds good."

I stole a glance at her while she scanned the song list. She really was a beautiful woman, her brown hair hung like a dark curtain around her shoulders and her blue eyes were vivid and alive.

I found myself appreciating her tiny frame and her small breasts as they strained against her tight, white t-shirt.

My eyes made their way back to her face to trace the curve of her pink lips.

"Are you checking me out?" she asked outright.

"Ah... um... *what*?" I stuttered, embarrassed at being caught out.

She turned to look right at me, our faces only a foot apart.

"I saw you." She raised her eyebrows at me. "And whatever you were thinking, you can stop it right there."

At least she's honest.

I rubbed the back of my neck. "So... you're pretty straight up, aren't you?"

She nodded and stared at me, still waiting for me to admit to checking her out.

"Yeah." I nodded. "I was. You're a good-looking girl."

"And what?" she asked.

"And what... what?" I asked, confused.

She laughed, obviously amused by my flustered state. "I'm not going to sleep with you," she assured me with a wide smile on her lips.

It wasn't until she said the words that I realized I would quite like to take this woman to my bed. She was beautiful, she was sassy and she was one of Quinn's best friends.

It was like the trifecta.

"You sure about that?" I asked with a smirk.

"One hundred percent... chicks before dicks."

I laughed loudly, and she joined in with a soft giggle.

Lexie Chase was funny.

I want her.

I'll have her.

I was going to sleep with this woman if it was the last thing I did.

I glanced over at Quinn, she was still talking on the phone. I owed her one big 'fuck you' and Lexie just might be the perfect way to do it.

Lexie shot me a knowing look that screamed 'it's not happening'.

Oh it's happening...

We spent the next thirty minutes crossing songs off the list and adding new ones. We didn't have time to rehearse anything so I was just going to have to trust that this girl knew what she was doing and hope that we wouldn't sound like a train wreck up there.

"Alright. I'm over this thing." Quinn slid her phone onto the table, startling the both of us.

"We're done anyway." Lexie smiled up at her.

"Good." She clapped her hands. "Let's decorate this bitch." Quinn grinned as she looked around the club.

3. Lexie

"Twenty minutes, Lex," Quinn called across the hallway.

"I'm nearly done," I called back.

I was staying at Harrison's house with him and Quinn. She didn't live here yet, but she seemed to spend most of her time here, and Logan currently had half of his house – where Quinn officially lived, pulled apart for renovations, so it was easier than us staying there.

I looked myself up and down in the mirror. My long dark hair was curled and pinned to one side and my red body-con dress hugged my small frame, stopping just below my knee with a small split up the front. I'd chosen the highest pair of heels I owned, a nude wedge, to give me some extra height – always being the shortest person in the room sucked sometimes.

I breathed in a nervous breath and checked my makeup one last time. It was flawless – Quinn did it for me, and she wasn't capable of anything other than perfection with a makeup brush.

This is the best it's gonna get.

I made my way downstairs and paused for a moment as I caught sight of Q and Harrison in a passionate embrace near the front door. He looked at her like she was the most precious thing he'd ever seen and she looked back at him like he was the only thing she'd ever need. I had no doubt that the two of them would spend the rest of their lives together – they'd be as happy as Lawson and Ellerslie were as husband and wife.

I smiled to myself as I thought about how much my two friends' lives had changed since they'd moved out here, they'd both had to survive their fair share of hurt, but they'd come out stronger and more in love than anyone I'd ever seen.

I hope someone will love me like that one day.

I smiled again as Harrison whispered something into Quinn's ear and nipped at her ear lobe with his teeth.

"Alright you two," I called out as I walked down the rest of the steps. "Keep it PG."

They broke apart with grins like teenagers that'd been caught making out.

"Wow. You look stunning, Lex... damn girl... that dress." Quinn appraised me from head to toe.

"Nah." I shook my head in disagreement. "It's just all this crap you put on my face," I countered.

Quinn rolled her eyes. "You don't need any of it," she insisted.

"Well then, why'd you put it on me?" I demanded with my hands on my hips.

Quinn looked lost for words for a moment before she realized I was joking.

She just makes it too easy sometimes.

I flashed her a 'gotcha' grin.

"I forgot how much of a little pain in the butt you are," she grumbled.

I laughed and shrugged unapologetically.

"Pot calling the kettle black, Skippy." Harrison grinned as he gestured for us to head out the door.

***

"Not to blow my own trumpet, but we did a pretty damn great job with this place," I stated as I looked around at the gold and white decorations Quinn and I had used to bring the club to life.

There were twinkling lights strung up across the ceiling, white table cloths with gold accents, huge bunches of white flowers, gold cutlery, and the stage was covered in lights and backed with sweeping white chiffon.

"It's gorgeous," El breathed. "You did amazing, Q." She reached out and squeezed Quinn's shoulder. "You too, Lex." She smiled at me.

"I just did what the boss lady said." I tipped my head in Quinn's direction.

Quinn's reply got cut off by Harrison sweeping her off her feet and twirling her around and around as she giggled. "You are far too good for me, Skippy," he told her as he set her back down on her feet, still holding her tight against his body.

I saw her blush as she shook her head in disagreement.

"Don't argue with me, baby. It's perfect. *You* are perfect."

I dragged my eyes off them, giving them some privacy as they shared a kiss.

I jumped at a throat being cleared right behind me and spun around as fast as I could on my sky-high shoes.

"Oh, Colt... hey..."

"Hey." He smiled. "You ready for tonight?" he asked as his eyes darted back over to where Quinn and Harrison still stood in a tender embrace.

"Yeah, I'm all set." I smiled back. "How about you, got your guitar tuned?" I pointed towards the stage – the opposite direction from his brother and ex-girlfriend.

He smirked, almost as though he knew what I was trying to do. "Sure have." He gestured for me to walk with him.

I looked him up and down. His black trousers and plain white button-down shirt looked good on him, he wasn't wearing a tie and he'd rolled his sleeves up – he was far more casual than Harrison and Lawson in their tuxedos, but he looked good, *really* good.

"You look nice," I told him. I knew I shouldn't be encouraging him; the way he was looking at me earlier had made it pretty obvious that he wasn't going to need much encouragement. But he was obviously having a tough time at the moment, and I wanted to compliment him when he deserved it, there was something about him that I liked.

His eyes darted over to Quinn and Harrison again – It was like he didn't even realize how often he was doing it.

He looked at me and chuckled. "I look underdressed."

His eyes roamed over my body, and I was embarrassed to admit to myself that it wasn't totally unwelcome. "You, on the other hand look absolutely stunning."

"Thank you," I replied quietly.

"No need to thank me, beautiful." He winked at me. I'd always thought that winking was a creepy-old-man trick, but somehow, when he did it, it was hot.

I knew damn well that he was trying to flirt with me to piss Quinn off; and I'd be willing to bet that he was planning to try and sleep with me to get even with her. The guy may as well have had Jason Derulo's 'X2CU' playing as his theme song. I let out a giggle at the thought.

Well if he wants to play games... I can play too...

"You just want to get into my pants," I accused, keeping my face serious.

His step faltered, and he turned to look me dead in the eye. He opened his mouth, then snapped it shut again, as though he was trying to decide whether to lie or tell the truth.

"So what if I do?" he finally answered.

"Then you're shit outta luck," I replied without missing a beat.

He took a step closer to me, getting right into my personal space – nearly touching me, but just not quite making contact.

I held back a smile – he was trying to mess with me.

"But am I really?" he asked in a seductive voice.

There's no way you'll beat me at this game, buddy.

I batted my eyelashes at him dramatically. "Um... well...I guess..." I sighed.

He swallowed deeply, waiting for my answer. He might have been trying to use me for revenge sex, but I knew he wasn't totally unaffected.

He leaned in closer in obvious anticipation.

"Yeah... you are *totally* out of luck," I replied, a grin breaking out.

"Damn you, Lexie Chase." He shook his head, finally realizing that I was playing with him.

I'm not finished yet.

"Now... if you weren't my friend's ex... well... *maybe* we could have worked something out." I reached out and ran my fingers over the collar of his shirt. I bit down on my bottom lip and saw his eyes dart down to look.

I leaned in closer to him and stood right up on my tippy toes so I could get near his ear. "But it's like I told you..." I whispered, so close that he would be able to feel my breath on his skin. "Chicks before dicks."

He chuckled as I pulled away, a shit-eating grin on my face.

He shook his head at his own gullibility.

I laughed along with him and batted him lightly on the arm. "So are you done with all this yet? I know you're only trying to piss her off." I tipped my head in Quinn's direction.

He grimaced. "Dammit. Am I that obvious?"

"You're entirely that obvious," I confirmed. "Plus, you do a terrible job of acting like an asshole. You're the token nice guy."

"Well shit."

"Yeah," I agreed with a laugh. "You've gotta stop looking at them though, it's giving you away," I teased.

"Alright." He nodded. "What else?"

"Don't bother calling *me* beautiful; you should save it for someone you might actually have a shot with."

He frowned at me. "But you *are* beautiful. I said that for your benefit, not hers – it's not like she was listening."

The look on his face told me he was completely serious, and for some reason I found my skin breaking out in goosebumps.

I blushed. "Okay." I cleared my throat awkwardly. "Well, um… *thanks.*"

He smiled and kept staring at me.

"Are you really still pissed at them?" I asked him bluntly. It was an inappropriate question, but I probably wouldn't see him again after tonight, so I didn't really care.

He shrugged. "Honestly?"

I nodded.

"Yeah… a little."

"A little is better than a lot," I pointed out.

He huffed out a laugh. "I guess that's true."

I patted his shoulder. "You'll get over it." I walked towards the stage to check the mic height.

"Are you sure you won't sleep with me?" he called after me, clearly joking.

I laughed and gave him the middle finger without looking back.

I heard his laughter echo through the large room.

4. Colt

It was weird, I was in the same room as Quinn and Harrison, yet I hadn't thought about them once since my conversation with Lexie. My attention had shifted, from one woman to another.

I was surprised by how funny Lexie was, she was as straight up as they came and she didn't appear to take any shit… she was the perfect distraction from my brother and Quinn.

Tonight was the first time I'd had to spend a long stretch of time with them as a couple, and I'd been freaking out about losing my shit over it. It wasn't as though I wanted Quinn for myself anymore, but I still felt pretty pissed at the world for the cards it had dealt me.

If I really thought about it, I was getting more and more okay with their relationship as the weeks went by. If I really wanted to admit it to myself, I was jealous of what they had together more than the fact that they were an item, I wanted someone in my life who would love me the way Quinn obviously loved Harrison.

I knew that sleeping with one of her friends wasn't going to give me what I really wanted, not unless I magically fell in love with her – and thankfully, Lexie was a smart girl who had talked me out of my stupid idea before I'd found myself turning into a man I didn't want to be.

"Two minutes, guys." Ellerslie popped her head into the back office and smiled at Lexie and then me.

"Thanks, El," Lexie replied.

"Kill it, girl." El winked at her. "And you make my girl shine," she told me with a good-natured grin.

"I'll do my best," I promised.

Without wanting to sound like an asshole, I was still a little bit skeptical of Lexie's abilities. I hadn't heard her voice and neither had Harrison, but he'd been told she was amazing. I trusted Quinn's judgment, but Lexie was just *so* small; I didn't know how it was going to work.

"So how much singing have you done?" I blurted out after Ellerslie left the room, trying my best to seem casual about the question.

She smirked at me. "You sound worried."

Failed at casual...

"Nah..." I lied. "I just haven't actually heard you sing... that's all."

"Well, you're about to," she called over her shoulder as she swayed her hips out the door. I grabbed my guitar and followed after her like a puppy dog; taking a good look while I had the opportunity to appreciate her sexy body without getting caught.

She really is stunning in that dress.

The crowd erupted into a chorus of clapping and cheering as Lexie was introduced and sauntered up onto the stage.

I grinned as I followed her up and took my spot on my stool; I settled my guitar in my lap and waited for her to signal me that she was ready to start.

"Thank you all so much, you're too kind," she cooed into the mic. "I'm Lexie, and this here is Colt." She turned and gestured to me. "He's been kind enough to play with me tonight."

I grinned and nodded towards the cheers in the crowd.

"Let's get this thing started, shall we?"

If the cheers and cat calls were anything to go by, the more formal part of the evening had gone well, and these suits were ready to unwind and relax.

She turned and nodded at me. "Ready?" she asked with an excited sparkle in her eyes.

She really is beautiful.

I decided then and there that it didn't really matter how well she sang, if it made her this happy, then that was the most important thing.

I winked and strummed the first cord to 'Titanium' by David Guetta and Sia. We had stripped it back and were doing an acoustic version.

Lexie turned back to the microphone and I heard myself gasp as she opened her mouth.

Her voice was absolute perfection; it floated through the room, strong, but somehow soft at the same time. My skin prickled with goosebumps.

The crowd went crazy.

It took everything I had in me to focus on the guitar in my hands and playing the chords she needed me to play.

She was *incredible.*

Incredible doesn't even cut it.

She belted out huge notes like they were child's play. Her voice stretched effortlessly through the last few notes and the crowd clapped and cheered – I found myself joining them.

I was completely mesmerized by her.

Lexie turned and giggled at my stunned expression.

"You're unbelievable," I mouthed at her.

She blushed and turned back to the crowd.

"Thank you, thank you, you're all very sweet."

She gave me a subtle thumbs-up and we started our next song.

She cruised through the next ten songs; 'Like I'm Gonna Lose You', 'Rockabye', 'Fast Car', 'Everglow', 'True Colors', 'Love Me Now', 'Human', 'Say You Won't Let Go', 'Shape Of You', and 'A Thousand Years'.

By this point she had the entire audience completely under her spell, and somewhere along the way she'd even started interacting with me, almost as though she were singing the songs to me. She'd gotten more and more playful as the set went on.

She belted out the last note, and the crowd burst into applause.

She came over and whispered in my ear. "Let's do that acoustics Hailee Steinfeld one I showed you, to finish."

I nodded, remembering the arrangement she was talking about. "The one with Grey and Zedd?"

She'd shown me a video of the acoustic version and it was amazing. Now that I knew what she was capable of, I couldn't wait to hear her sing it.

She grinned and nodded enthusiastically.

"Whatever you say, my little song bird," I teased her.

She made an excited noise and went back to her mic.

I chuckled. She was freakin' adorable.

And talented...

And captivating...

I looked up at her and my eyes landed on her perfect ass.

And sexy...

Shit...

I like her.

She turned back around and gave me her cute little 'are you ready?' face where she screwed up her nose in the sweetest way.

Oh hell... I like her...

I needed to snap out of it. I had to really focus for this one.

The song was 'Starving'. There was a lot of guitar work involved in it and we hadn't originally planned to include it in the set, so I hadn't rehearsed it at all. I smiled to myself; the fact that she'd asked to do it now meant that she trusted me not to screw it up.

I gave her a wink.

I'm ready.

I ran my fingers over the strings.

Her voice was like an angel's. I'd never heard someone sing this well, live, and completely unaided by auto tune and all that shit they used these days.

Lexie didn't need it.

She should be on the radio.

She took the mic from the stand and swayed her body to the more upbeat tune.

I laughed as the beat picked up and she strutted over to me and sang the song to me, tapping a tambourine to the beat on her slender hip.

She looked and sounded so fucking good, up here killing it, shaking her ass and hitting every note. Her smile and bright blue eyes lit up the entire room, but all I saw was her.

Perfection.

Shit.

I want her.

I might not have wanted her to spite Quinn anymore, but damn it, now I wanted her – just for being her.

5. Lexie

We bowed and ran off the stage together laughing like teenagers. We busted into the back room, giant grins on both of our faces.

"That was so much fun," I panted, out of breath from all the excitement.

"That was incredible." Colt pulled me in for an unexpected hug, and I found myself wrapping my arms around him too, holding him close.

"Thank you so much for playing for me," I murmured against his chest.

He didn't seem to be in any hurry to let me go, and surprisingly enough I didn't seem to want to let him go just yet either. Being in his arms felt comfortable... it wasn't at all like hugging a stranger should have felt.

Our vibe up there had been amazing. I'd never had a connection with someone on a stage like that before. He knew exactly how to play for my voice – when to slow down... when to speed up, he knew just how hard to push it. He was either an incredibly talented musician who could read any singer he played for like a book, or he'd felt the same connection I had up there.

Or both...

He released me with a sigh, but one of his hands lingered lightly on my upper arm.

"You have the most amazing voice I've ever heard," he told me, complete honesty in his voice.

We were standing only inches apart and it still seemed too far.

Something had happened up on that stage... we'd *clicked*... I just had no idea what that meant would happen now.

"Thank you," I replied quietly. "You were pretty great yourself."

He looked down at me and tentatively reached his hand out for a strand of hair that had escaped my pins. He swept it gently from my face and behind my ear.

"Perfect," he whispered.

I was so nervous; butterflies were going crazy in my stomach.

"I don't know what's going on here right now," he confessed, his voice husky. "But I'd really like to kiss you."

God, I want that too.

"What about Quinn?" I asked timidly.

He shook his head. "It's not about her anymore... I'm not sure it ever was." He dipped his head closer as his eyes burned into mine.

He's gorgeous...

Could I...?

"No."

I can't.

"She's still one of my best friends." I sighed and looked down at my shoes.

I wanted to get closer to him, but I knew I couldn't – I couldn't do that to Quinn.

"I can't. I'm sorry," I whispered.

He reached under my chin and tipped my face up to look at him. "Don't be sorry." He gave me a small smile. "She's lucky to have such a good friend."

He kissed my forehead softly and my stomach did one of those silly flips.

"If you change your mind..."

Quinn chose that exact moment to push the door open. "Oh my god! You guys were insane out there! I couldn't belie—"

She froze the moment she saw the two of us, standing too close, Colt's hand still on my bare skin.

"Oh hell. Sorry... I just wanted to thank you both. I'll... I'll see you out there..." she stammered as she tried to turn around to leave.

I stepped back from Colt quickly. "Don't be silly." I reached for her and hugged her tight. "That was so much fun, thank you for letting me sing."

Quinn pulled back and tried to search my face for answers. "Thanking me? Oh hell no. I owe you big time. You're even better than I remembered, Lex."

You wouldn't be thanking me if you knew what I'd wanted to do just now.

"Thank you... I actually... I need the bathroom; I'll be out soon, okay?" I stumbled through my words as I pushed past her, not bothering to wait for a reply.

I felt like a fraud.

What kind of friend am I?

Chicks before dicks.

Chicks before dicks.

I chanted it to myself all the way to the bathroom.

***

I heard the door swing open, and I sat quietly, waiting for whoever it was to leave. I'd been hiding in here for fifteen minutes, and I needed at least that much time again to regroup and get my shit together.

"Are you coming out, or am I coming in?" she almost drawled.

Shit.

I should have known Quinn wouldn't just leave it alone.

"What do you mean?" I squeaked.

Shit. Shit. Shit.

Smooth, Lex, real smooth...

"I'm not mad." I could almost hear Quinn rolling her eyes.

"You're not?" I cringed at my still too squeaky voice.

She tapped her foot impatiently. "Just get your ass out here," she demanded.

I cautiously stood up off the closed lid of the toilet and unlocked the stall door. I shot her a sheepish grimace as we came face to face with one another.

She rolled her eyes in typical Quinn fashion, just as I suspected she would have been doing.

"Spill it, Lex." She crossed her arms over her chest.

"Okay, just don't be mad... it was nothing," I insisted. "*Nothing* happened... I swear."

"Lexie, for God's sake, just get on with it, we're missing the party."

Just get it out.

"He wanted to sleep with me – to piss you off." The words burst out. "I said no." I held my hands up to emphasize my point.

The corner of Quinn's mouth twitched with what I thought might have been a grin.

"He joked about it earlier, we had a laugh and I told him to give it a rest... and we were good."

Quinn rolled her head around in a circle and gestured with her hand for me to wrap it up.

"Then we went on stage... and it was incredible..." I sighed.

"It was amazing," she agreed.

"And I don't know... something changed up there." I blushed. "I mean he's *gorgeous*, but I knew that beforehand... I'm not sure..." I shrugged. "I guess we made a connection." I wrung my hands together nervously, waiting for her reaction.

"And out there just now?" she prompted.

"Nothing happened," I insisted quickly. "He said he wanted to kiss me."

"So why didn't he?" she asked, her head tipped to the side, watching me carefully.

"I stopped him; I said I couldn't, because of your history with him."

"Did you want to kiss him?" she asked simply.

I looked at her for a beat and weighed up my options before deciding that I needed to be honest – this was one of my best friends.

"Yeah," I admitted. "I did... I'm sorry, Quinn." I sighed and looked down in shame. "But it doesn't matter, I'll go back home and I'll probably never see him again," I mumbled.

"Lex?" Quinn said with a giggle.

I looked back up at her, she was grinning like a fool.

What the...

"The fifteen minutes it took me to get here?" she prompted.

"Yeah...?" I answered, not sure what she was going to say next.

"I was pumping all of that information out of Colt." She smiled proudly.

"What? You were?" I gaped at her.

She nodded and smirked.

"Then why'd you need to drag it all out of me?" I demanded.

She mused over her answer for a moment. "Let's just say for experiment's sake."

"*Quinn...*" I warned. "You better tell me what you're talking about."

"He's over me!" she shrieked, jumping up and down like an excited little kid.

What?

I was so confused.

Quinn must have seen it on my face, because she carried on her explanation. "Colt *finally* looked at me without hurt in his eyes. He didn't try to make me feel bad, and he seemed genuinely happy."

She was visibly elated by this realization; I however, was totally confused.

"That's great, but I don't see why you're bringing it up now." I looked to her for another explanation.

"Oh... sweet, little, Lexie." She reached for me and squeezed my shoulders. "Colton *likes* you... and you like him." She raised her brows at me. "The two of you have a little somethin'-somethin' going on."

"He just wants to sleep with me," I stated.

She shook her head slowly. "Colt's not like that."

"He *told me* that's what he was trying to do," I insisted, even though I had a feeling that his harebrained scheme was long forgotten by now.

"I know. I heard him yelling after you earlier."

I went to tell her 'I told you so', but she didn't give me a chance.

"But he never would have gone through with it. He's too nice... he'd never use a woman like that."

I thought about it and realized she was right. He was a nice guy and I had a feeling he would never set out to intentionally hurt anyone.

"Look, all I'm saying is that he's interested. I'm not mad, hell, I'm not even a little bit mad, and if you want to see where it goes, or even just have a little bit of holiday fun, then you should." She said it as though it was exactly that simple and uncomplicated.

"But he's your ex," I stated.

"He's hardly my ex," she scoffed. "And besides, the fact that I'm in love with his brother probably cancels out any right I'd have to be pissed off. Agreed?"

She's got a point.

I swallowed deeply. "Agreed."

"Good." She frowned. "I will warn you though, Colt can get..... *attached*... so just be careful."

My stomach did a little flip of excitement at the thought, but I pushed it down. I barely knew the guy.

We got caught up in our on-stage chemistry, that was all.

Now I just needed to convince myself of that.

"Alright... I'll keep that in mind."

"Oh..." Quinn shot me a grimace. "There might be one other *teeny tiny* little obstacle."

"What?" I murmured nervously.

"Harrison's friend Jake was pretty smitten with the sight of you... he wants an introduction."

My mouth gaped. "Seriously? I go months and months without a second glance – five minutes in this place and I'm already getting hit on."

Quinn rolled her eyes like she didn't believe me as she tugged on my arm and led me out of my hiding place.

"Welcome to the jungle." She laughed as we walked into the crowded room.

6. Colt

"Jake Roscoe can fuck right off," I snarled at Harrison as I watched his childhood friend falling all over Lexie.

The poor girl had barely set foot in the room when he'd swooped in and monopolized her attention.

She had been looking at me too, our eyes had locked and we'd had that whole silent communication thing going on.

Then cue the jackass...

I watched her; she was chatting with Jake, but every so often she'd look over to me and smile shyly when she realized my focus was still entirely on her.

Harrison looked back and forth, following my line of sight.

"Ohh I get it now... you're hot for Lexie."

I growled as Jake put his hand on her forearm.

"Did you just growl?" Harrison asked with a chuckle.

"He fuckin' touched her," I hissed by way of explanation.

"Maybe she wants him to touch her," he taunted me.

"Fuck off, Harrison."

"You got a mouth on you when you're pissed off, don't you?"

I pulled my eyes from Lexie and looked over at my older brother. "Seriously? Are you trying to make me mad?"

"Nah." He shook his head. "I'm trying to get you to grow a pair and go get the girl." He smirked.

His stupid, smug face was only making me more agitated.

I'm not letting this one go.

I gave Harrison the finger and stalked off in the direction of Lexie.

She spotted me coming and her whole face lit up. I grinned back at her.

Jake doesn't have a shot.

I slid in next to her and slipped my arm around her waist. She leaned into me gratefully, so I decided to push my luck and kiss the top of her head.

"Hey," she whispered.

"I was wondering where you'd got to," I replied softly.

I looked up, acting like I'd only just noticed who she was standing with.

"Oh, hey, Jake, how's it going, man?" I reached out and he shook my hand slowly. "I see you've met Lexie?" I smiled down at her.

"Yeah..." he trailed off. "I didn't realize... ah... look, I'll catch you later. Nice to meet you, Lexie." He turned and stalked off into the crowd, his disappointment obvious.

I chuckled. I couldn't exactly blame him for being disappointed; Lexie was a total knock out.

It was probably immature of me, but I didn't give a shit. Jake was a big boy, he could handle getting out-played.

"You made him think we were a couple." Lexie nudged me in the ribs with her elbow in a halfhearted attempt to tell me off.

She'd made no effort to move away from me, and I was pretty happy about that. My hand felt right at home resting on her slender hip.

"You got a problem with that?" I grunted as I pushed my luck and tugged her in close, slipping my other arm around her too.

She blushed and a small gasp fell from her lips. She shook her head.

"Good," I stated. "Because I like you, my little song bird."

She giggled.

"I want to take you out on a date."

I knew she had felt guilty about the Quinn situation earlier on, but I'd spoken to Q myself, and she'd assured me that she would give Lex full permission to do whatever she wanted.

I knew that based on morals, I probably should have been resisting her – a bigger man would have. But I had a sneaking feeling that when it came to this particular woman, I'd be whatever kind of man it took just to have her.

I just have to hope she wants this too.

"I don't know if that's a good idea." She sighed, frown lines appearing between her eyes. "I go back home on Friday..." she trailed off.

"Let's just take it one day at a time," I offered. "You could be a total diva, and I might decide to cut you loose anyway."

"I *am not* a diva." She raised her eyebrows at me. "Why do people keep calling me that? If a coffee hasn't been stirred in a clockwise direction, it's just not worth drinking, right?" Her face was dead serious.

Oh shit. Maybe she is...

My eyes bulged. "Umm... I mean, I..."

"Gotcha." She grinned.

I huffed out a breath. "That was not funny." I chuckled as I placed another kiss to the top of her floral-scented hair. "Let's go get a drink, you little smartass."

"Just one condition for the date..." She stopped me before I could lead her towards the bar.

"Anything," I answered quickly.

"I would really like to see more of this city," she replied with a small smile.

I already had a plan forming in my mind, and her request just made it all the more perfect.

"That, I can do," I replied.

***

I swallowed deeply and tried to subtly adjust the bulge in my pants.

Jesus.

Watching Lexie Chase dance was hot as hell.

She'd been out there shaking and grinding for a good half hour. Calvin Harris and Rihanna's hit 'This Is What You Came For' was blasting through the sound system, and the girls were all out there cutting loose. I wanted to join her more than you could imagine, but these dress pants were entirely useless at hiding what she was doing to me.

We'd hit the bar earlier, had a few drinks and shared a few stories. It was the strangest feeling; I felt like I already knew her so well, like we weren't strangers at all.

Lexie had talked about her life back home and I'd hung on her every word. She worked as a singer on a cruise ship, and it was obvious from the look in her eyes when she talked about it, that she lived for her job.

Reeve sauntered over and bumped his shoulder against mine. "You've got it bad."

I chuckled and nodded in agreement without taking my eyes off Lexie. "Is there anything that girl can't do?"

"Ummm... drive a car?" he offered.

"What?" I turned to look at him. "She can't drive?"

He laughed. "Nope. She rides her bike everywhere."

"That's ridiculous. She's twenty-two years old," I replied in disbelief.

Reeve shrugged. "It is what it is."

"I'm gonna teach her."

I decided right then and there that I was going to teach that woman to drive before she got back on that plane.

It's the perfect excuse to spend time with her.

He just grinned in response.

"It's good to see you smiling again, Colt." He clapped me on the shoulder. "I know you didn't want anything bad for them, but still, you deserve happiness too."

I didn't even need to ask what he was referring to – it was obvious. And he was right. I never wanted anything but happiness for Harrison and Quinn, but it had still been a tough pill to swallow.

"Yeah thanks, Reeve," I choked out. "I appreciate it."

He started to walk away, but turned back to me. "And maybe if a few hours with Lex was all it took for you to move on, then Q wasn't ever the one for you anyway."

He wasn't entirely right. It'd been a few months alone, and then a few hours with Lexie... but that didn't matter. The point was right. Quinn wasn't, and never would be the one for me. She was Harrison's and he was hers. It was as simple, and as complicated as that.

I glanced back out at Lexie and couldn't help but wonder what would happen now. She'd agreed to a date with me tomorrow – and she didn't know it yet, but I'd be keeping her for the entire day.

I had a deep-seated desire to know everything there was about that girl, and I wasn't going to stop until I did.

7. Lexie

"So what's the deal with you two?" El's eyes twinkled as she regarded me curiously.

We'd been dancing for ages and I needed a break and another drink.

"Two waters please," I told the bartender.

I looked back over at El. "Honestly... I don't know." I nibbled on my bottom lip. "I don't even know him... but I'm having a really hard time not throwing myself at him." I grinned.

Having a few drinks had definitely loosened me up.

"He is gorgeous," El agreed as we both looked over at Colt.

He was talking animatedly with a guy I didn't know. He had a big grin on his face and I couldn't help but smile as he threw his head back in laughter.

"*So* gorgeous," I agreed.

"So go for it," El encouraged.

"From what I've heard, that's the exact advice you gave Q, and look how that turned out." I shook my head in amusement.

"Yeah... that was *unfortunate*." El grimaced. "I told her to just have some fun, but poor Colt didn't get the message." She sighed and looked over at Colt fondly. "He's a really nice guy, Lex, he was so good to us when I had those issues with that stalker, he really kept an eye on Quinn."

I reached out and squeezed her arm, it was a long time ago now, but I knew El didn't really like talking about it too much.

"I think that was part of the problem. Lawson was so protective of Q and I, and you know what she's like... there's no forcing her into anything. So Lawson pushed... and Q ran to Colt to get away. They spent a lot of time together over that period that they probably wouldn't have otherwise. I think that's when Colt caught the feelings," she explained.

I laughed. "Caught the feelings – I like it."

"I'm certainly not giving you the same advice." She giggled. "But it couldn't hurt to get to know him a little better. He's really sweet, I like him and it'd be nice to see him happy again."

"But I'm only here for a few more days," I replied softly.

"Just take each day as it comes?" she suggested.

"That's what he said." I smiled as I glanced back over to where Colt stood. He was looking directly at me now and still talking to the same guy.

"I'd bet you one hundred dollars that he's talking about you right now," El told me.

Colt's arm lifted and he pointed right at me.

"See," she boasted.

"That's her..." I saw the words form on his lips from across the room.

My heart fluttered.

Oh lord.

Quinn and El were right. Colt was a great guy, and there was no reason not to go for it and see what might happen.

***

I spent the rest of the night dancing with El, Q and a few of their other friends. Even Lawson had joined his wife on the dance floor.

And holy hell.

That man could move.

If it wasn't for the fact that he was married to one of my best friends, I probably would have thrown myself at him – El had laughed so much she'd nearly cried, and Quinn had screwed up her nose and pretended to gag when I'd accidently mentioned that thought aloud.

It appeared that Harrison and Colt weren't of the dancing variety. No amount of begging, pleading or coercing seemed to be able to get them out on that dance floor.

I was willing to bet that Colt wasn't as bad as he was insisting he was – the way he played, rhythm obviously flowed in his veins, but I didn't push it. He seemed to be more than happy sitting back and enjoying the show.

We'd put back more drinks than was in any way necessary and I'd laughed until my face hurt. It was the most fun I'd had, off of a stage, in a really long time.

I'm so glad I came to see my girls.

The other reason I was glad I'd come was currently approaching me with a cheeky gleam in his eyes.

"Are you having fun, my little song bird?" He slipped his arms around my waist when he reached me – the same way he had several times tonight, and my arms instinctively went around his neck.

It had only been a few short hours, but it was somehow already a familiar gesture. It was sweet, and sexy, and I liked it more than I knew I should.

"You know... nicknames are meant to be shorter than the person's name... not three words longer," I stated playfully.

He chuckled. "Says who?"

"I dunno." I shrugged. "The nickname rulers."

"The nickname rulers can suck my d—"

I clapped my hand over his mouth before he could finish his sentence.

"Rule breaker," I stage whispered.

He laughed behind my hand and nipped at my finger with his teeth.

I pulled my hand back and smiled up at him – all the way up... we were going to look utterly ridiculous standing together if I ever wore flats.

"Are we still on for tomorrow?" I asked casually as I reached up and wrapped my hands around his neck again.

"You bet your sweet little ass we are," he replied quickly.

"Where are we going?" I quizzed. I needed to plan an outfit.

"I'm not telling," he replied, his voice smug. "But you only need to bring yourself," he added, almost as though he could read my mind.

"Can I wear heels?" I pondered aloud.

"Ahh... no." He laughed. "Probably wouldn't be a smart choice."

"But I'll look like a midget next to you," I whined jokingly.

"You'll look perfect." He reassured me as he placed a soft kiss on the top of my head, the same way he'd been doing all night.

"What time should I be ready?" I sounded giddy and excited, but I didn't care. I *was* giddy and excited.

"I'll pick you up at eight."

"So, a late dinner...?" My stomach nearly growled at the thought of waiting that late. I liked to eat.

He laughed, and it was such a perfect sound that it took me a minute to realize I'd said something that he obviously thought was funny.

"What?" I crinkled my nose up at him, wanting to be in on the joke.

"Not eight at night." He tapped my nose. "Eight in the morning," he amended.

I gaped at him.

Is he serious?

I flicked my watch towards me. It was three-eighteen.

"You can't be serious?" I replied quickly. "That's not even five hours away, Colt," I added when all he did was grin, with his stupid, beautiful, hazel eyes glowing like caramel.

"You're right." He dropped his hold on my waist and grabbed one of my hands. "It's not worth waiting, let's just go now."

I giggled at his obvious joking as he dragged me out of the room and down the hallway.

"Colt!" I cried out between giggles.

"C'mon," he insisted, tugging my arm harder to speed me up.

"Where are we going?" I tried to pull my arm back, a huge grin on my face.

"That's it," he warned before hoisting me up over his shoulder and carting me further down the hall.

"Colt!" I could hardly get the words out, I was laughing so hard. "Put me down, you thug!"

"That's no way to talk to your date," he mock scolded as I bounced around on his shoulder, my face at his back.

"What in the name of God…"

I heard Quinn's voice and did my best to look up. She was standing at the end of the hallway, down where we'd come from, and she had a huge smile on her face.

I waved to her as Colt stopped, opened a door, walked in, and sat me down on my feet. I glanced around – we were in an office – *his* office, if I had to guess.

"Well this is no place to take a date," I teased, still looking around.

My heart thumped in my chest at the realization that we were all alone once again.

I heard the door shut and I swung around to look at him. His eyes were filled with heat and lust.

"Lucky I've got better plans for the real thing," he told me as he beckoned me to him with his finger.

I went straight to him and tilted my head up, wanting what I was sure he was after too.

His lips crashed down on mine, and I knew I'd been right about his intentions. He wanted this as badly as I did.

My hands went around his neck at the same time that his found my waist.

We were a tangled mess of lips, tongues and teeth. We were drunk and sloppy, but it was still the most electric kiss I'd ever experienced.

"Lexie..." he murmured against my lips when we finally broke apart.

"Mmm hmm," I answered.

He pulled me in close, and I let my arms fall down around his waist. He rested his chin on the top of my head. "So perfect," he whispered as he hugged me tightly to him.

"You're such a charmer," I replied.

He shook his head softly. "It's true," he insisted. I could hear the smile in his voice.

"It is inconceivably *untrue.*" I sniggered. "You've only known me a few hours... spend some time with me and you'll see the light."

"Alright, alright... I'll spend time with you. You don't have to hound me, woman."

I rolled my eyes at his goofy grin.

He let go of me and checked the time for himself.

"I guess I'd better let you get some rest." He grabbed my hand again, opening the door and leading me out, back the way we came.

I didn't even reply. I just giggled like a school girl and followed after him.

The thought occurred to me that I trusted him... *completely*... he probably could have taken my hand and I would have followed him anywhere.

How can I trust him entirely already? I barely know the man...

What am I doing...?

He looked back at me over his shoulder and shot me a breathtaking smile.

That is what I'm doing.

My concerns faded away the moment his eyes landed on mine and his sexy lips curved up into that grin.

Have a bit of fun.

I just needed to relax, let go, have a good time, and see what happened.

I'll take my own advice for once.

Colt took me right back to where El, Q, Harrison and Lawson were waiting, knowing smirks on all of their faces.

"You ready, girl?" Q asked with a wink.

I blushed and tried to pull my hand from Colt's.

He flat out refused to give it up, instead bringing it up to his mouth and kissing my knuckles softly.

"I'll see you at eight?" he said it like a question, but I knew he wasn't going to take no for an answer, and more importantly, I didn't have any desire to say no to him anyway.

I want to see him again...

I nodded.

"Wear comfortable clothes and shoes," he added with a smile.

"Dammmmn girl." Quinn let out a low whistle. "Active wear in a few hours? We better get you home to bed."

The others all laughed, but I barely noticed them, I was busy with the handsome man in front of me.

"I'll see you tomorrow." I promised him.

He leaned in slowly, giving me plenty of time to move if it wasn't what I wanted, and placed a soft kiss on my lips. I wasn't going anywhere. He pulled back and I waited for him to nod and let go of my hand before I walked towards my friends.

I sighed as his touch faded from my skin.

Quinn slung her arm over my shoulder. "Well now, tell me all about it, little one," she said as she patted my arm playfully.

8. Colt

God I hope she doesn't think this is stupid.

I glanced at the clock for the millionth time and watched the numbers flick over to eight AM.

Finally.

My eagerness to see her had resulted in me arriving to my brother's house fifteen minutes early. I was so pumped to spend the day with Lexie.

I'd gone home right after they'd left the club last night, leaving the duty manager to close up, and I'd even managed a few hours' sleep, which was all I really needed anyway.

Hopefully Lex isn't a ten-hour-a-night kinda girl.

Only one way to find out...

I swung open my car door and stepped out on to the driveway. I walked slowly towards the front door, contemplating whether to ring the bell, or use my key. I didn't want to risk giving Lexie a fright, but I also didn't want to feel the wrath of Quinn, from being woken up early on a Saturday morning.

That woman is like a hibernating bear.

I grinned to myself, and my step faltered as I realized I'd just thought about Quinn in a totally new light. I wasn't bitter, or jealous, or angry.

God that feels good.

I turned my keys over in my hand, looking for the key I had to Harrison's door.

"Lost something?"

Her voice surprised me and I dropped my keys. I swooped down and snagged them off the gravel.

I looked up at her and my breath caught in my throat. She looked beautiful. She had on black tights, a zip-up fleece, Nikes, and her hair was tied back in a loose ponytail. She had a big bag slung over her shoulder.

I noticed all that in the flash of a second it took for me to work my way up her body and lock my eyes onto hers. She'd cleaned all the makeup from last night off her face, and I was mesmerized by the sight of her smooth complexion and bright blue eyes.

Eyes shouldn't be that blue...

I could feel myself getting lost in the deep pools.

She's spellbinding.

"Why are you looking at me like that?" she asked abruptly. "Is there something on my face?" She started wiping at the sides of her mouth with the sleeve of her jumper.

I stood up straight and grabbed at her hand before she did some serious damage to her pretty face.

"Stop," I instructed. "You're perfect."

She stopped trying to pull her hand back and smiled shyly up at me.

I pulled her in closer and used my free hand to tip her head up to look at me. I was a full head taller than her.

I grimaced. "I'm so sorry."

"What? Why?" she asked, confused.

"I see why you wanted to wear heels," I told her solemnly.

"You're a dick," she said with a laugh. "I get it; I'm the size of a hamster."

"C'mon." I tugged at her hand. "Let's go buy you one of those little running wheels for your cage."

She mock punched my arm with a laugh and let me lead her to my car.

***

"We're here," I announced.

I stifled a laugh as I watched her confused expression take in the deserted parking lot.

"I don't get it," she stated after a minute of thinking about what we could possibly be doing here.

I laughed loudly at her expense and got out of the car. I rounded the front and opened her door for her.

She still looked confused as hell, but she took my offered hand and stepped out.

"Just come with me," I told her as I led her back around the front of the car.

"What are we doing here?" she asked with confusion.

"Here," I replied, handing her the car keys as I gestured for her to sit in the driver's seat.

"Oh... um..." She blushed. "I... actually, I can't drive," she admitted.

"I know." I smirked. "Reeve told me...and I decided that you're not leaving until you learn."

"What?" She gaped.

"You heard me. I'm teaching you to drive."

Her eyes bulged.

"I don't care if it takes the whole week," I told her with determination in my voice.

"This is a really nice car, Colt... what if I break it?"

"You won't," I reassured her. "And besides, it's insured," I added with a wink.

A slow smile spread across her face. "Alright then." She nodded.

"Yeah?" I asked in surprise. I'd been expecting a little more of a fight.

"Yeah," she confirmed. "But it really might take all week." She pouted. "I'm a *terrible* driver," she added in a flirty voice.

She stepped into me and reached up to hold on around my neck. My arms found her waist and pulled her flush against me.

"You know what? I bet I'll need lessons. Every. Single. Day," she admitted. "And maybe I'll be really bad and you'll just have to spend hours and hours with me." She sighed dramatically. "Are you up for that?" She grinned.

Oh hell yes.

"Does a bear shit in the woods?" I replied.

She frowned. "Well, I guess so?"

"Well then..." I bent down and lowered my lips to hers and brushed them lightly. "I guess I'm up for it."

***

Jesus. Christ.

When Lexie pouted those sexy lips at me and told me she was a terrible driver, I'd thought she'd been exaggerating.

She wasn't.

She was undoubtedly the worst driver I'd ever encountered – and that included the time I got in the car with my fourteen-year-old neighbor when we were in high school.

The steering, stick shift and foot pedals had been about two things too many for her to manage at one time and we'd ended up bunny hopping around that lot, stalling over and over again, for forty minutes before she'd thrown in the towel.

"You could have at least let me try an automatic," she scolded me. "It's my first time in years, for God's sake," she muttered under her breath as we drove—me behind the wheel—to our date destination.

I couldn't stop myself from laughing at her; she was so damn adorable when she was flustered. Her cheeks were pink and her eyes were wide.

"Stop laughing at me!" she cried in mock outrage. "I wasn't *that* bad." She crinkled up her nose and burst out laughing at the ludicrous statement she had just made.

I raised my eyebrows at her.

"Okay, okay," she admitted. "I was terrible."

I shook my head in amusement.

"In my defense, I did warn you." She pointed her finger at me.

And yet, I wasn't prepared...

"You'll do better tomorrow," I reassured her.

Her mouth fell open. "You *can't* be serious?"

I frowned in confusion.

"You don't really want to endure that all over again do you?" she asked in disbelief.

I pulled into the car park of the ferry terminal and turned the engine off.

"Not really," I told her honestly, turning to face her. "But I told you that I'd teach you, and I will."

She opened her mouth to argue, but I cut her off.

"As long as I'm getting to spend time with you, I'm not complaining," I promised as I took her hand in mine and lightly kissed her knuckles.

"You're being incredibly kind to me."

"What can I say?" I bragged. "I'm just that sort of guy." I winked and jumped out of the car.

I grabbed our bags, and her door swung open and she jumped out to meet me.

"We'd better hurry up or we'll miss our ferry," I told her as I took her hand in mine.

"Where are we going?" she asked excitedly.

"You wanted to see the sights?" I grinned at her. "Well here we are."

9. Lexie

I glanced over at Colt, the wind whipping through my hair, and knew without a doubt that I'd never felt quite this free.

Sure, I lived half of my life on a boat, but this was different. It was just for the sake of it. No one here knew me, or expected anything of me. Hell, even Colt didn't really know me, not all of me anyway.

But it feels like he does...

I was having an amazing time with him. He'd told me about his brothers and his parents, and about the town they grew up in. He wasn't close with his parents, neither were his brothers, and my heart broke for him.

My parents were separated, and both re-married, but that had just doubled the love I'd had growing up. Being an only child and having no siblings to share things with was the only thing I considered a downfall of my childhood.

Colt had smiled and laughed as I'd told him stories about my crazy dad, Mike, and his equally kooky wife, Viv. My mom, Sally, was quite the opposite; she was always the practical one, that's probably why she was so much happier now with her husband of ten years, Alex, than she ever was with my dad.

Colt had even talked a bit about his ideas for the club, and while he did seem passionate about his visions, it didn't sound like he had been investing the time required to make much progress lately. Of course I'd opened my big mouth and pointed that out to him... he'd just shot me a knowing smirk, and said nothing more about it.

Then, we were on the deck of the ferry, being taken to a place I'd never even heard of, let alone visited.

Colt smiled one of his smiles that had my stomach flipping and gestured with his finger for me to follow him inside. I snapped another quick picture and followed after him. He took a seat near the front and patted the cushion next to him.

"Pass me your phone," I instructed as I sat down next to him.

"What for?" he asked curiously as he pulled it from his pocket and handed it over.

I reached into my backpack and pulled out a pair of earbuds. "We're going to see what kind of music you like."

"Shit," he muttered under his breath as he took the earbud I was offering and slipped it into his ear.

I opened his Spotify and chose the playlist he had last played. I scanned through the songs.

"*This* is your playlist? Jesus." I shook my head at him. "Are you kidding me?"

He grimaced.

"That's pathetic. It's like heartbreak hotel in here. Snap out of it, kid."

"Who are you calling kid?" He smirked.

"You." I jabbed my finger at his chest. "These songs reek of a fifteen-year-old boy."

He laughed deep and loud.

"You actually follow a playlist called 'Broken Heart,'" I hissed as I continued to scroll through his music library.

He attempted to defend himself. "I *was* broken hearted."

"You were something alright," I mumbled to myself. "There's One Direction in here," I gasped, completely outraged.

He leaned back in his seat and chuckled. "What can I say; I'm a closet boy-band fan."

"You a closet anything else?" I sniggered as I found some decent music and hit play.

"With you sitting next to me?" He raised his brows. "Hell no."

I laughed at his lighthearted teasing.

"Unless Zac Efron makes an appearance," he joked. "Then I'm gonna have to love ya and leave ya."

"Huh," I mused. "I picked you as more of a Justin Bieber kinda guy."

He nodded his head and thought hard. "He's a close second."

I giggled. The banter between us was fun and easy.

"You wanna know a secret?" he whispered as he moved in closer to my ear.

I nodded slowly. Goosebumps formed on my skin at his nearness, I could feel his breath fanning across my neck.

"I'm actually the kinda guy that's into the sexy little brunette woman sitting next to him." His voice was hoarse.

"I bet you say that to all the girls," I breathed when I couldn't come up with anything witty to say.

"I do," he agreed. "But the eighty-year-old lady I sat next to on the bus didn't seem to appreciate it too much."

I swatted his arm and rolled my eyes.

Clown.

He leaned back against the seat and slung his arm over my shoulders, tapping his foot to the beat.

He touched me so casually, as though he had the right to already. I didn't mind, not one bit; there was a familiarity between us I couldn't explain. I'd known him for less than twenty-four hours, but I was already well aware that he was something special.

"We're here." He smiled down at me, breaking me from my thoughts.

He stood up, slinging the huge, suspicious-looking bag he had brought along, and my backpack onto his shoulders.

"I can take that," I protested as I got to my feet.

He just laughed at the suggestion and took my hand in his again.

***

"This is incredible," I told him for the one hundredth time.

"I think you said that already," he drawled.

He was reclined on the picnic blanket he'd brought along, and I was leaned back against him, the picture-perfect view of the horizon stretched out before us.

"But it's just *so* pretty," I replied.

He chuckled. "Well, I'm glad you like it."

"I do." I nodded. "It's perfect."

He couldn't have chosen a better date. The ferry had taken us to a small tourist Island; we'd strolled around hand-in-hand before hiking up to view the city and have the picnic lunch that Colt had prepared.

He's thought of everything.

I tilted my head back to look at him and smiled at the sight. He'd surprised me by pulling out a pair of black-rimmed glasses and removing his contact lenses – I didn't even know he'd been wearing them. He'd explained that his eyes were getting irritated. Apparently he didn't like wearing the glasses, he didn't think they suited him... but I wasn't in agreement.

I hadn't realized that glasses could look so... *hot*.

"What?" he murmured, looking down at me and sweeping a strand of hair away from my forehead.

"Nothing." I shook my head. "I'm just enjoying finding out what kind of guy you are," I replied in a soft voice.

"And what kind of guy is that?" he asked, his fingers tracing gentle patterns across my cheek.

"The kind of guy who packs every different food group because he's not sure what I like," I told him with a smile.

"I know now," he replied with a triumphant smile, as though knowing what kind of sandwich filling I enjoyed was like winning a contest.

He's just so sweet.

I smiled shyly. "And the kind of guy who's not afraid to say how he feels, or go after what he wants," I continued, my voice a hoarse whisper.

He nodded, his eyes locked on mine.

"And the kind of guy who looks too hot for his own damn good, especially wearing those glasses."

He huffed out a disbelieving breath.

"It's true," I insisted. "And you're patient, and sweet, and kind, and—"

He cut me off, claiming my lips in a flash.

His mouth was hot and demanding, firm and persistent. I kissed him back with a passion I didn't know I possessed, and I felt a little bit of my heart start to belong to him. He kissed me like he was never going to get another chance – and the truth was he might not.

He might not...

The reality that we lived so far apart came crashing down on me and I felt tears welling in my eyes.

Sensing my change of emotion, he pulled away slowly.

"Hey, what's wrong?" he asked, lifting my chin to look at him when I tried to avoid eye contact.

"I'm sorry," I blurted out. "It's just... I live over two-and-a-half-thousand miles away."

He searched my eyes, his fingers clasping my jaw.

"I know I'm being silly." I shook my head and felt a tear escape and roll down my face. "But I like you. I *really* like you already."

"I feel the same way," he told me without hesitation.

"But what's the point?" I shrugged, my voice breaking at the end. "I'm going home on Friday, and then I'll be there and you'll be here. And we won't be together," I rambled.

"Lex..." he whispered. "Don't think like that."

"I don't want to set myself up to get hurt," I whispered before he could say anything more. "And I can feel it already. If we keep doing this, I know I'm going to be broken in six days' time."

He nodded slowly, accepting the truth in what I was saying.

This decision was killing me, but I knew myself well, and I knew that if things carried on this way, this good, I could very well be in love with this man by the time I needed to board that plane.

It's better this way.

"I wish more than anything that we could give this a shot," he replied, his voice thick with emotion.

He pulled me against his chest and held me tight.

"Me too," I whispered back.

"Do you want me to take you home now?"

I shook my head. "Not yet?" I pleaded. "I just want to pretend that we have forever for a little while longer."

***

I pushed the door shut and leaned back against it, tears welling in my eyes.

My heart was screaming at me to go back out there and tell him that I'd made a mistake, but my head was telling me that it was better this way.

I won't get hurt this way... if only that were true.

I was already hurting, and we'd barely even started anything yet.

I took a deep, steadying breath and headed towards where I could hear TV in the living room.

"You're back already," Quinn acknowledged with a frown as I came into view. She was sitting on the couch reading a book, Harrison's feet in her lap.

"Yeah." I nodded, a fake smile plastered on my face.

She narrowed her eyes at me. "What's with the face?" she demanded.

"What face?"

"Don't give me that shit." She eyed me up, head to toe. "Something's wrong."

Dammit.

I'd forgotten just how much Quinn saw. It was like she had a knack for seeing through the bullshit.

She turned to Harrison who was sprawled out on the couch, mindlessly flicking through TV channels. "You." She pointed at him. "Out."

He smirked at her. "Bossy."

"You like me bossy," she teased, lightly shoving his feet off her lap.

He sprung up from his seat with the grace of a wild cat. "What'd my idiot brother do now, little Lex?" He mussed my hair as he strolled past me.

"Nothing," I mumbled. "And don't do that, I'm not five years old, I'm just short," I called at his retreating back, my retort all bark and no bite.

"What happened?" Quinn demanded, pulling my attention back to her.

I dropped my bag to the floor with a thud and moved to sit down next to her. I tucked my feet up and got comfortable. If I knew Quinn, and I did, we'd be here until she got all the information she wanted.

"Nothing happened," I told her. "Nothing *bad* anyway."

"Then why have you got a face like a smacked ass?"

I frowned at her. "I take offence to that."

She waved her hand dismissively. "Doesn't make it any less true."

I fiddled with the bracelet on my wrist.

"I really like him," I told her quietly.

"I know," she replied. "But I don't see why that has you nearly in tears."

The mention of tears had my eyes welling up all over again.

"It's... it's just..." I stammered. "Oh what's the point, Quinn? He lives here, and I don't. What's the point of taking it any further? I'll just end up getting hurt."

Quinn nodded slowly. "So you don't want to see him again?"

"Of course I want to," I replied quickly. "I just can't."

"That's bullshit and you know it," she snapped.

I looked her in the eye, a little shocked at her tone.

"What's the worst that could happen, Lex?" she asked, more gently this time.

I shrugged. "I dunno... we have an amazing week together, I fall in love with him, and then I have to go back home, alone."

"So, let me get this straight... your *worst-case* scenario is falling in love?"

"No, it's falling in love and then having to walk away," I clarified.

Quinn gave me a small smile. "You know, when I first realized the extent of my feelings for Harrison... I was terrified. I was worried that he wouldn't feel the same way, or that his loyalty to his brother would be too much for us to overcome, or that I'd lose myself in loving him... I was terrified."

"It all worked out okay for you." I smiled.

"It certainly hasn't been smooth sailing, but we're here now and I couldn't be happier with my choices."

"Why do I feel like you're telling me this for a reason?" I raised my eyebrows in question.

She smirked. "Because I *am*... it's like El says, nothing that's worth it ever comes easy."

"But I'm leaving in—"

"I know you are." She held her hands up in defense. "All I'm saying is if you really think you're okay with never seeing him again, then fine. But if you have doubts... then you should think hard about it. I don't want to watch you living with regret."

I nodded. I needed some time to absorb Quinn's advice.

"I'm gonna take a shower." I stood up and headed for the door, grabbing my bag on the way.

"Good idea, Lex."

***

The water pounding down on my back must have done the trick to clear my head.

What was I thinking?

If this was meant to be – really meant to be, then it'd work out. I just had to take a chance...

I know what I need to do.

I jumped out of the shower and dressed in a rush. I flew down the stairs, my hastily packed bag clutched in my hands. I burst into the living room, expecting Quinn to be where I'd left her.

"Quinn?" I called out.

"Yeah?" she called back, her voice coming from the direction of the front door.

"Do you think you could..." I trailed off as I saw Quinn, a massive grin on her face and her car keys in her hand.

"What?" she asked. "Could I drive you somewhere perhaps?" She had a smart look in her eyes, daring me to admit that she had been right.

"Yeah, yeah, you were right." I rolled my eyes.

"Course I was." She smirked. "Now get your ass in that car."

"If you can love the wrong person that much, imagine how much you can love
the right one."
- Author unknown

10. Colt

I took a swig of my beer and flicked through the channels again. I don't know why I was bothering; I couldn't focus on anything on the screen anyway – all I could think about was her.

I was probably overreacting.

I barely even know the woman.

It felt like I knew her though. I felt like I'd known her my whole life... and the fact that it was over before it even got the chance to begin really fucking sucked.

I understood her decision, and I could see why she wanted to protect herself. But it was going to be a long six days, knowing she was only a short drive away, but I couldn't see her.

Suck it up...

I was always the guy that could never take a hint, never give up when it was over – Quinn was a prime example of that. But I wasn't going to do that this time. I couldn't, not to Lexie. I respected her too much to try and make things hard for her, no matter how much I wished it could be different. I wouldn't risk her getting hurt, not when she'd asked me not to.

I took another long pull of my beer.

Move on.

Step one: get drunk.

The buzzer sounded on the intercom.

Pizza's here.

I jogged over to the panel and held down the button to let the delivery guy up.

Pizza and beer. What more could I need?

The answer hit me like a ton of bricks as I swung open the door and came face to face with the woman who had taken over my every thought.

"Lexie?" I glanced up and down the hallway, looking for some explanation as to how she had appeared here, literally on my doorstep.

"Quinn dropped me off," she offered by way of explanation. "And then you just buzzed me up without even asking who it was – you shouldn't do that you know… I could have been a murderer," she scolded me.

"I was waiting for pizza," I explained lamely, showing her the twenty bucks I had tucked in my hand. I couldn't think of anything else to say, the surprise of her sudden appearance had turned me mute.

She smiled and looked right at me, waiting for me to acknowledge what was right in front of me.

She shifted her weight nervously, and I noticed the full bag she was carrying.

She came back…

"Is that… are you…?" I stuttered hopefully.

She smiled again and bit down on her lip. "If you'll have me?"

I'll have you alright…

I grabbed her and roughly pulled her against me, our lips meeting in a crash of passion and heat.

Her tiny body pressed against mine and I hoisted her up so I didn't have to bend down to meet her.

She let out a giggle.

"I thought I'd never see you again," I growled against her lips.

"Me too." She sighed. "We've only got six nights together; so we better make them count."

That I could do.

I turned us around and Lexie clamped her legs around my waist. I walked us into my apartment, kicking the door shut as I went. My hands were cupping her ass, and I let go with one to snag her bag and toss it onto the couch.

"Your place is nice," she murmured even though her eyes had been locked on mine the entire time.

"You want the tour?" I ground out, hoping like hell that she didn't.

She shook her head slowly and bit down on her full bottom lip. "No," she whispered. "I want you to take me to bed."

"Thank fuck for that," I growled.

Her light laugh filled my ears as I carried her through the living room, down the hall and straight into my master suite.

I didn't stop until my shins hit the side of my king-sized bed. I lowered her down so she was on her back beneath me.

"Lexie," I choked out, my voice strangled and coarse.

"I'm here," she cooed.

"I missed you," I replied. It was a bizarre thought, but it was one hundred percent true. I felt like I'd been missing a part of me.

She smiled at me looming over her and reached for the hem of my shirt.

I am totally and utterly screwed.

"I missed you too," she replied softly as she lifted it up over my head and tossed it aside.

She made a purr deep in the back of her throat, and I knew I was a total goner.

11. Lexie

Colt without a shirt on was truly a sight to behold. His body was tight and toned... the grooves of his abdomen pronounced and firm.

I'd never seen anything so tempting.

My eyes on his bare flesh spurred him into action. He tugged my Nikes off my feet and tossed them behind him without a second thought. My yoga pants came off next and were disregarded in the same manner.

I sat up and pulled my top up over my head.

"I'm in heaven," he mumbled to himself.

I reached for his sweat pants and tugged them roughly down his legs.

Holy hell.

Colt had gone commando.

I reached forward to take him in my hand but he jerked his hips back.

"Oh no, little bird, you touch me like that and I'll lose it." His hazel eyes looked lighter – the gold more pronounced, and they were burning bright with desire.

I pouted, but leaned slowly back against his bed, resting on my elbows, just drinking in the spectacular sight in front of me.

He kicked his pants off fully and stood in front of me, naked as the day he was born. He was hard and ready, his dick standing proudly at attention in front of him.

I licked my lips.

"Jesus," he muttered. "You are gonna *kill* me."

I giggled softly as he reached slowly for my underwear and slid them down my legs and over my feet.

He held them tightly in his hand as he stood before me, taking his fill of my body.

Eyes on my skin had never felt so intimate, so erotic.

"Damn, Lex," he groaned. "I can't promise I'll be able to take this slow."

I didn't want it slow. I sat up again and slowly unhooked the clasps on the back of my bra, letting it fall forward revealing my breasts.

"Screw it," he mumbled as he lunged for me, lightly knocking me back onto the bed.

His mouth found mine with an urgency that had me trying to catch my breath. His tongue slipped into my mouth, one firm brush after another against mine.

He was supporting his weight on his elbows, leaving just enough so I could feel his body against mine.

He was hot and hard against my leg and I couldn't wait to feel him inside me.

"I need you," he groaned.

I needed him too. There was no need for foreplay; just his hot stare on my bare skin alone had me ready to go.

I reached between us and gripped his erection. He was hard as a rock.

He let out a deep shudder and I knew he was as close to the edge as I was.

I guided him towards me and felt the tip of him press gently where I needed him most.

"Colt," I groaned, begging him to take the lead.

That was all the coaxing he needed. He thrust up into me in one movement and I let out a moan of pleasure.

God, it feels so good.

He stilled inside me momentarily and a hiss escaped his lips. "Damn, Lex," he groaned before tilting his hips back and thrusting into me again.

I moaned in satisfaction.

"More," I demanded.

He gave me more.

He picked up his pace, finding a rhythm that was both punishing and pleasing.

I lifted my hips to meet him stroke for stroke, and he grunted out his appreciation.

I was so worked up I could barely breathe. His eyes were boring holes into mine, like with every thrust he was edging closer and closer to my soul.

I couldn't look away.

My hands gripped his back, the firm muscles flexing under my fingers.

"I want you to come for me," he panted. "Now, Lexie, I want you to come *now*," he demanded, still looking into my eyes.

I was so close.

He broke our eye contact and dipped his head to suck on my neck. He devoured the skin there like a staving man would a juicy steak.

He moved further down to my breasts, taking one of my nipples into his mouth and sucking hard.

So close.

I let out a long moan as I felt my orgasm building, almost to the point of release.

He dragged his teeth over the hard peak, and I lost it; pleasure exploded through my body, coming in fast, hot bursts that had me thrashing and moaning.

"Colton…" I moaned.

He mumbled something incoherent in my ear before picking up his pace to an even more grueling speed.

His whole body tensed. I knew he was close. He had to be, my body couldn't take much more of this pleasure.

He let out a guttural moan and thrust deep and hard, one last time before stilling inside me.

"That was… wow." I murmured after a few moments of heavy breathing.

He huffed out a breath. "*Wow* doesn't even come close."

I stroked my finger softly down his face and smiled up at him.

He pressed a sweet kiss to the tip of my nose. "Let me just take care of the condom."

He slid out of me and I realized our mistake at the same moment he did.

There is no condom.

The look of horror on his face filled me with dread.

"Lexie, babe, please tell me you're on the pill."

My heart hammered in my chest as I shook my head slowly at him. "I'm not."

"Shit, god, I'm so sorry, I've never been that careless, I swear." His voice was strained and full of remorse. The look on his face was pure terror.

"It's okay," I reassured him, even though I felt anything but calm myself. "We'll take care of it… and I'm clean, I promise," I told him quickly.

His eyes softened. "I didn't mean… I know you are, Lex, you're not that kind of girl."

He was right – I wasn't.

Until right now.

"I've *never* had sex without a condom," he promised me in return. "And I had a check not too long ago anyway."

"Okay... good... this is good," I said aloud – for his benefit or mine, I wasn't sure.

"But what do we do now?" he asked, still slightly panicked, and rightly so.

"I'll get a morning-after pill tomorrow?" I suggested. "I've just had a period a week or so ago, so I think it should be fine... I didn't really listen in sex education..." I rambled. "Maybe we won't take the risk?" I offered finally.

He looked almost torn for a moment.

"Yeah, okay," he agreed, seemingly more relaxed now. "I'll take you to get it tomorrow, alright?"

I nodded in agreement, and he grabbed a towel from the chair next to his bed and handed it to me to clean up.

"What went through your head just now?" I asked him gently, my curiosity getting the better of me.

He smiled sheepishly. "You caught that, huh?"

"You're too easy to read," I told him with a smile.

He lay down next to me and tucked me close against him.

"I don't want to send you running..." He shrugged. "And I'm not crazy enough to be wanting a baby right now... but I was just imagining how beautiful a little mini you would be."

My heart thumped in my chest. "But your face was horrified?"

"Because I was careless with you," he explained. "I should never have put you in a position where you needed to take a pill because I forgot a glove."

"It's not like I was exactly worrying about consequences either... it's not all on you," I insisted.

"It's my dick – it's my job to wrap it," he argued.

We locked eyes in a silent standoff.

He won when I lost it laughing.

"Alright, you wrap your dick from now on," I agreed with a grin.

"Will do." He saluted me like a soldier.

"Thanks for not totally freaking out." I placed a kiss on his collarbone. "Most guys would have been spewing."

"Well I'm not most guys," he assured me.

He leaned in and kissed me softly on the lips.

"No, you most certainly are not," I murmured as he moved on, kissing the skin below my ear.

He rolled me slightly so he was above me again, his mouth trailing a path down my neck and finding its way to my breast. He teased and sucked and nibbled until I was squirming.

"This time I'll use a condom," he promised.

12. Colt

"I need to feed you," I groaned as I rolled over and reached for Lex.

We still hadn't left the bedroom. We'd alternated between sex and sleep for the past three hours. I didn't know about her, but I was exhausted and half starved. The pizza had eventually arrived, but still sat disregarded on the bench, stone cold by now.

"Mmmmm... I... mmmm..." Lexie hummed incoherently into the pillow.

I chuckled. "You're delirious."

She rolled over to face me. "It's all the sex," she groaned dramatically. "My body isn't made to withstand all this pleasure."

"What else have you got for me? My ego isn't quite big enough." I grabbed her and pulled her tight into my arms.

"Well, I'll tell you something that *is* big enough," she quipped as she snuggled in.

I barked out a laugh. "Now I know you're lying."

"Well I can't comment on the average of the population, but I can tell you, Colton Hunt, that yours more than meets the minimum requirements."

"Your vagina has minimum requirements?" I enquired.

"Of course she does, what kind of ship would she be running without a set of standards to adhere to?"

This girl is a total loon.

I chuckled loudly. "You refer to it as a girl?"

She perched up on her elbow, eyebrow already raised as she looked at me. "Would you refer to your junk as anything other than a guy?"

"I can safely say I've never thought about it," I replied with amusement.

"Well you should," she insisted as she snuggled back down.

"You're funny," I told her as I stroked her bare arm. "I like talking to you."

I felt her smile against my chest. "You like the *talking*, huh?" She snickered.

I prodded her lightly in the ribs. "Don't get me wrong, I'm not opposed to the rest of it. But I'd be content to just lie here, holding you and talking, Lexie, believe me."

"Me too," she replied softly. "I feel like I've known you forever."

I knew exactly what she meant.

"How has it only been…" I glanced at my watch. "About thirty hours?"

"I've never slept with someone I've only known for thirty hours," she murmured.

I wish I could say the same.

I didn't sleep around, but I'd had a couple of one-night stands in the past. They didn't really do it for me – sex without emotion wasn't really my thing.

"I'm glad to be your exception," I replied.

"And it's not like this is a one-night stand…" She trailed off, clearly fishing for some kind of confirmation that I wasn't just in it for a onetime thing.

"If you think I'm letting you out of my sight for the next six days, you are bat shit crazy, little lady."

Don't freak out, don't freak out…

She peeked up at me and smiled brightly. "But what if I need to pee?"

That's my girl.

I pretended to think about it. "I guess I'll allow it. But if you're in there longer than five minutes, I'm breaking the door down."

She giggled at our nonsense banter.

"I might never leave." She sighed.

I had a pretty good feeling that by Friday, I was going to wish that were true.

***

After my shower I detoured to the kitchen to throw the cartons from the Chinese food into the trash and grab the open bottle of wine from the fridge.

I walked back into my room to find Lexie sprawled out across my bed on her belly, my shirt barely covering her ass and her legs crossed up in the air.

She had some kind of book opened in front of her and an assortment of other crap scattered all over the place.

"What's all this?" I asked curiously.

"It's my planners," she replied without looking up.

"Planners, *plural*?" I questioned.

She gestured to the books that I hadn't noticed at first.

"Okay… how many planners does one girl need?" I asked cautiously.

"Oh, sweet, innocent, little Colt," she teased. "Nobody has just *one* planner."

"Alright..." I resigned myself to being schooled on the world of planners. I sat the wine down next to our half-empty glasses. "Fill me in."

"Okay," she replied excitedly.

I couldn't help but grin back, her excitement was infectious.

She reached for a small, purple book. "This one is for work." She flipped through the immaculately decorated pages with coordinated script mapping out her work shifts.

"This one is for plans with friends... novels I read..." She flipped through the stack of books. "I have more at home... one for bills, one for trips I take..."

"You're out of control," I murmured as I reached for the one she was working on. "What's this one for?"

She blocked my hand and didn't answer. When I looked back at her, she was blushing.

"Lex, what's this one for?" I grinned.

"It's not really a planner..." She trailed off. "It's more like a journal."

I glanced down at the page she had open and spotted my name in her flawless handwriting.

"I saw my name." I pointed at the page. "Now you have to tell me what it's about."

She smiled shyly. "I was making a page for the past day..." She held it up to show me.

She'd drawn a little picture of a car with a big red warning symbol next to it. I laughed. She'd also drawn a boat and written 'the perfect island' in the shape of a hill. My name was written over and over around a drawing of a mic and a guitar.

"This is amazing," I told her genuinely.

"You don't think it's too high school?" she asked as she screwed up her adorable little button nose.

I shook my head. "I think it's perfect."

"I brought this with me too." She smiled as she pulled out the Polaroid camera I'd seen her snapping pictures with earlier in the day.

"Did you get some good shots today?" I asked.

She bit down on her lip. "A couple," she answered vaguely.

"Can I see?" I prompted.

I could see her thinking about whether or not she was going to let me see them.

"Turn back a page," she instructed and gestured to the book I was still holding.

I flicked the page back and smiled as I took in each image. I was in every single one of these pictures. Even the one of the city's skyline had my hand pointing something out in it.

"They're all of me," I commented, my heart beating fast in my chest.

"Yeah..." She cleared her throat and I knew she was embarrassed.

She'd been taking pictures when I hadn't even realized she had her camera out.

I smiled when I reached the selfie she'd insisted we take at the top of the track. We were lying on the picnic blanket, my arm was around her and her body was curled against mine. Our smiling faces looked back at me.

I tugged the photo gently off the page. "I'm keeping this one." I told her.

"Hey!" She swatted my arm. "Now I've got a gap."

"Take another one." I suggested as I reached over and tucked the photo into my bedside drawer.

"Fine." She pouted.

I stacked up her books and sat them down on the floor next to the bed, still thoroughly amused that she'd bothered to bring them all with her.

I tugged her arm and she fell on top of me, her back against my chest, the camera still in her hands.

I swept her long, dark hair out of the way. "There. Take a picture."

"I look like I've just had hours of sex," she protested.

Jesus...

"Good," I growled. "Maybe I'll keep this one too."

"Fiend." She giggled.

"Take the picture, Lex."

She held her slender arm up in the air, the lens pointed at us. "Say cheese," she instructed.

There was no way I could resist the temptation of her neck right next to me.

Screw the smile.

I tucked my face into her neck and nuzzled, breathing her in. She giggled right as I heard the click of the camera.

"You were supposed to smile," she scolded me with all the authority of a bag of cotton candy.

"I couldn't help it," I replied by way of defense, still kissing the soft skin along her jaw.

She pulled the small photo from the back of the camera and waved it around, waiting for the image to process.

She giggled again as I found a sensitive spot on her neck and she wiggled free from my hold.

She tucked the camera back into her bag and sat back down next to me, cross-legged on my bed.

I'd never seen a sight so perfect. Having her here felt so right... seeing her in my shirt, hair mussed and eyes bright...

I could get used to this.

If only that were possible.

I pushed all thoughts of her leaving out of my mind. I was jumping the gun, something I always did.

Only this time it feels right.

I leaned up and kissed her lips softly.

She closed her eyes momentarily, savoring the contact.

I took the opportunity to snag the photo from her hands.

"Well that was a dirty trick," she grumbled.

I laughed lightly and turned my attention back to the Polaroid, the image was appearing before my eyes. I swallowed deeply as it became clearer.

She's so beautiful.

She was stunning. Her bright blue eyes looked right at the camera, her smile was mid laugh and as genuine as they came, her dark hair was splayed across my chest and I was utterly absorbed in her, my eyes closed, like she was the center of my universe.

It was perfect. We couldn't have taken a better picture if we'd tried.

"I'm *definitely* keeping this one," I choked out, still clutching the photo in my hand.

"Let me see," she murmured, holding her hand out for it.

I held out the picture for her to take.

She gasped as she looked at it.

"I know," I replied to her unsaid words.

She looked up from the photo and stared at me, her eyes full of passion.

I beckoned her to me with a crooked finger.

The photo fell to the bed as she rushed towards me on all fours, looking like the sex vixen she was.

I tugged her into my lap and clasped her face gently. "It's just you and me, little bird."

"I like clingy. I like double texts, phone calls, good morning & goodnight texts. I like knowing someone cares. I like knowing they try."
- Author unknown

13. Lexie

"How'd it go?" he asked the minute I settled back into his beautiful car. Colt drove a white Mercedes... I liked it, it suited him... it was a hot car.

I still can't believe he let me attempt to drive it.

Good." I smiled brightly, holding up the bag I'd been given in the pharmacy. "All sorted."

"Did you take it already?" he asked.

"Nah, she recommended I take it with food so I don't get sick, so I'll take it at lunch."

He reached over and tugged on my buckled seatbelt before starting up the car and indicating to pull out into traffic.

"Why do you do that?" I asked him curiously. I'd noticed he'd done it each time I'd put it on. "Is it broken or something?"

He glanced at me out the corner of his eye, shooting me a look of disapproval. "Do you really think I'd let you use a faulty seatbelt?"

Not judging by the look on your face...

I shrugged. "Why do you keep checking it then?"

He stopped at a set of lights. "Just making sure you're safe," he replied, a slight blush staining his cheeks.

I didn't know what to say to that. What I'd thought was some odd quirk was actually a really sweet, unexpected gesture.

I reached out and gave his knee a grateful squeeze. "Where are we headed?" I asked, looking out the window at the unfamiliar surroundings.

"Harrison's," he replied.

My heart dropped.

"Oh, okay... well I left my bag at your place," I confessed awkwardly. "We'll have to stop in and get it."

He laughed and reached for my hand, intertwining his fingers with mine. "Did you think I was kidding when I told you I wasn't letting you out of my sight?"

I frowned. "But then..."

"We're going to Harrison's for two reasons," he explained. "Number one, to get the rest of your stuff... and number two, because I'm a little afraid of what Quinn might unleash on me if I steal *all* of her time with you."

I smiled wide. "You make a good point." Today was Sunday and probably the last day I'd have to spend with my friends. El and Q both had work tomorrow; running a business didn't happen on its own.

"Wait, why do we need my stuff?" I quizzed him. I was staying at Harrison's...

Wasn't I?

He shot me a sheepish grin. "Well I guess I should actually ask you and not just assume... but, ah... I was wondering if you maybe might want to come and stay with me?"

He wants me to stay with him?

"The club is closed until Wednesday anyway... and I can just go in and do the bare minimum this week." He ran a hand through his hair and I could tell he was nervous. "So I'm free as a bird... and everyone else will be at work all day..." He trailed off, waiting for my reaction.

"You really want me to stay for another five nights?" I asked in surprise.

It wasn't nearly enough time, not with how perfect yesterday, last night and this morning had been, but it was all I had. And I wanted to spend it with him.

"Shit yes I do," he confirmed without a moment of hesitation.

"Then I'm in." I squeezed his hand. "Shot gun *not* being the one to tell Q." I sniggered.

He chuckled, his eyes on the road. "Don't worry, babe, I'll protect you."

I knew he was just teasing, but it was true. He'd taken me to the pharmacy and I knew he felt genuinely terrible about the situation we'd gotten ourselves into. He'd fussed over me, made sure I was comfortable and content all morning, and last night too.

We'd stayed up late, watching a movie in bed, so tangled up in one another it was hard to figure out where one of us ended and the other began.

I must have fallen asleep during the movie, because I woke this morning, the clock telling me it was half past nine, to the smell of bacon cooking and coffee brewing.

It was heaven.

The fact that Colt had been cooking in nothing but an apron and a pair of boxer briefs just made it all the more appealing.

I sighed softly thinking about it.

He's gorgeous.

His body was *perfect* – in my opinion anyway. He was lean and toned and firm in all the right places. His body was like a well-oiled, fluid machine. He called it a runner's body. I was shocked that running was the only thing he did to keep himself looking that good.

Colt had a body that looked like it was built to do bad things.

"You think she'll flip?" he asked as he turned into Harrison's drive.

He startled me; my mind was back in the kitchen with a half-naked Colt.

"I'm not sure." I shrugged. "She'll either be all for it, or dead set against it. There's not a lot of in-between with Quinn sometimes."

"I think she'll be cool." He decided as he pulled the car to a stop.

"Only one way to find out," I mused.

***

"Hoooonnnneeeyyyy, I'm hoooommmmeee," I called out as I swung the front door open.

Colt chuckled behind me.

I reached for his hand and tugged him along next to me.

"Get in here you little horn dog, I want details," Quinn yelled from what sounded like the kitchen.

I snorted out a laugh. If Quinn had a filter, she very rarely used it.

"Maybe I'll wait in the car," Colt deadpanned, pretending to turn and head back out.

"Not happening, Hunt, we're in this together." I tightened my grip on his hand and dragged him with me into the kitchen.

Quinn's eyes lit up when she saw I wasn't alone. She was sitting on the bench, sucking on a lollipop and Harrison was throwing some toppings on a homemade pizza base.

Thank god one of them can cook.

"Well hello there," Quinn drawled. "How is the happy couple this morning?" she asked, a curious gleam in her eye.

"We're both good," I answered quickly. I knew Quinn was sounding us out. She was looking to see if we'd deny her 'couple' label or not. I wasn't fazed by it, and judging by the size of Colt's grin, neither was he.

"Sealed the deal bro... knew you were smarter than you looked," Harrison taunted his brother.

"That's quite the compliment coming from the domestic goddess over there," Colt threw back without missing a beat.

"You can talk. I've seen that apron you wear," Harrison retaliated.

I nearly choked on my next breath as dirty thoughts of Colt making my knees weak wearing that very apron filled my mind.

I felt my face blush scarlet as I coughed and spluttered.

"You okay, Lex?" Colt asked, obviously concerned with my sudden outburst.

I coughed again. "I'm... fine," I spluttered.

He frowned and tried to rub my back.

"I'm good," I said, more clearly now. "Ugh, I just... it just... went down the wrong way," I explained lamely.

Quinn was looking at me with an amused smirk.

"So what's been happening?" she asked casually.

Sex, sex, more sex, eating, some more sex...

"I've just been getting to know your girl here." Colt looked down fondly at me as he answered her.

I smiled back up at him. It was hard not to. Colt had this... *presence*. He was bright and glowing.... he exuded happiness and light. All I had to do was look at him and I wanted to smile too, he just had that kind of an effect on people.

"I can see that," Q replied, her voice amused.

I could feel a full interrogation coming on.

"Skippy," Harrison warned. "Leave them alone."

I laughed.

Quinn pouted. "No one left me alone when I was falling in love with you," she grumbled to him.

Falling in love?

I'm not falling in love... am I?

I didn't know the definite answer to that question and that realization was more than a little frightening after only such a short period of time.

"So, ah... the reason we came by... is... I... umm..." I stumbled through my words.

"Spit it out, Lex," Quinn prompted.

For God's sake, I'm a grown woman.

"I'm gonna stay with Colt for a bit... Is that okay?" I asked nervously. I felt like a teenager asking her parents if she could spend the night at her boyfriend's place.

Quinn and Harrison exchanged knowing glances. Quinn held out her hand to him with a shit-eating grin on her face.

"*Dammit*," Harrison mumbled. He reached into his pocket, and pulled out a brown leather wallet. He counted out fifty dollars and slapped it into Quinn's waiting palm.

Quinn giggled gleefully and slipped the bills into the back pocket of her jeans.

"What the hell was that all about?" I asked when it became apparent that neither one of them was going to provide any explanation for their transaction.

"She bet me fifty bucks you'd have fallen for his charms already," Harrison explained as he slid the pizza he'd made into the hot oven.

Quinn smirked. "He thought you'd be able to hold out at least two days." She rolled her eyes, as though the thought was ludicrous.

Shit heads...

"I don't know whether to be flattered you had so much faith in me, Quinn, or wounded that my own brother didn't think I'd be able to get the girl," Colt joked, not the least bit bothered by their little exchange.

"So anyway..." I interrupted their little ball-busting session. "I'm gonna go grab my stuff..."

"Oh no you don't," Quinn replied quickly, jumping down from the bench and making a beeline for me. "I'll let you go without a fight, but not until later. I need girl time," she begged.

I looked over at Colt and he smiled and winked, telling me silently that he was more than happy to stay.

I was relieved. I wanted to spend time with Quinn too, but I hadn't expected him to be so comfortable here.

"So what's for lunch?" I asked with a grin.

"Yesss!" she replied. "He makes the best pizza, you'll love it." She tipped her head in Harrison's direction.

I half listened to her rambling on about the secret ingredient Harrison added to his sauce until Colt tugged me into his arms.

"The pill," he whispered in my ear.

Shit.

"Should I just take it with dinner?" I whispered. I really didn't want to attempt to sneak it in here right now – not with hawk-eyed Quinn around.

He smiled and nodded in agreement.

"Come try this," Quinn called to me from the cooktop.

I squeezed Colt's bicep and gave him a soft kiss on the lips before going to see what all the fuss was about.

***

"So... on a scale of one to ten, just how smitten are you?" Quinn asked, with a look that said 'don't even bother trying to lie to me'.

I bit down on my lip nervously. "About an eight and a half," I admitted.

"Eight and a half out of ten... way to go, Colt," she announced.

I shushed her. I didn't want him to hear us talking about him.

"Relax." She rolled her eyes. "They went out to the garage to look at Harrison's new deathtrap of a motorcycle."

I let out a relieved breath. It wasn't that I didn't want Colt to know how much I liked him, but I was worried I'd frighten him off if he heard that, this early into our relationship.

If I can even call it that...

Quinn laughed. "He wouldn't run scared you know."

I narrowed my eyes at her – sometimes it was like she could read my mind.

"No?" I asked cautiously.

She shook her head. "He's not one to shy away from feeling things, Lex, if anything he probably jumps in too quickly."

Disappointment coursed through me. "So this kind of thing is normal for him?"

Quinn's eyes softened. "Not at all."

I relaxed slightly.

"Shit, I'm sorry if I made you think he does this sort of stuff all the time..."

I raised my eyebrows at her. That was exactly what she'd made me think.

"I think he's just very open to finding love," she amended. "I'm not saying that he falls in love with every person that he meets," she reassured me quickly. "But I do think that he gets ahead of himself, and leaves himself open to being hurt, but he has good intentions."

"So I'm not just another notch on his bed post?"

She huffed out a laugh and shook her head. "He's not like that."

I nodded my head. I guess this wasn't really new information to me, Colt had told me as much himself. It was just different hearing it from someone else.

"I think when he's met someone that he really does love, he'll realize the mistakes he's made in the past," she added with something that sounded like hope in her voice.

"Is this too weird?" I blurted out. "You know, me seeing a guy you've dated?"

Quinn sighed. "It's only weird if you make it weird, Lex," she replied simply.

I studied her for a moment and decided that I wasn't going to let it bother me. It was just one of those things that had happened, and everyone had moved on from.

"For what it's worth, he seems pretty smitten with you too." She smiled.

I had to smile about that.

***

"Well that was actually quite fun," Colt commented as we pulled out of Harrison's driveway.

"It was." I smiled in agreement. "You sound surprised."

He chuckled quietly. "Well yeah, I can't say I'd ever imagined hanging out with a girl I used to date, who is friends with the girl I'm currently seeing... and then there's the fact that said ex is now in big time love with my brother..." He chuckled again. "So yeah, I'm surprised."

I grimaced. "You make a valid point."

I had thought that there may have been some kind of awkwardness with the four of us spending the afternoon together, but there hadn't been.

Not at all.

Quinn had been genuinely interested to find out what had happened between Colt and me, and if anything, she was eager for him to move on.

She already had, after all.

Colt had seemed to cope being around Quinn and Harrison just fine. The two of them had gotten more comfortable showing affection in front of him as the day wore on and I'd even noticed Colt smiling when Harrison had whispered something in Quinn's ear and made her blush like a school girl. It was a massive transformation from the Colt I'd witnessed in their presence on Friday night.

"It was good." He smiled out the window. "I missed feeling like this."

"Like what?" I asked softly, studying him as he spoke.

"Happy... you know, *content*," he answered after a beat. "I got so caught up in the hurt and the... I guess you could say betrayal." He nodded. "Yeah, I definitely felt betrayed, by both of them."

His confession damn near broke my heart.

"Anyway, I was so caught up in it, I couldn't see it... I couldn't see how good they were together. I couldn't get over myself long enough to realize it wasn't their fault that they came into each other's lives when they did. If they'd met six months earlier it would have been an entirely different story."

"It's hard to find perspective when you're hurting," I told him sympathetically.

He nodded in agreement. "And I guess the fact that I can see it now is testament to the fact that I'm finally over it."

"I'm glad."

"It's a lot to do with you, you know that, right?" He shot me a smile before looking back at the road.

I was overjoyed at the knowledge that meeting me had helped Colt to kickstart his life again, but I was also worried.

What happens when I leave...

I must have had my thoughts written all over my face.

"What's wrong?" he probed.

"I'm just worried you've replaced one hurt with what will eventually become another."

He reached for my hand and pulled it into his lap.

"It's not like that at all, when I say you helped me move on, it's because you helped me see that Quinn wasn't right for me. You pulled me away long enough for me to finally see that I was holding on to something that never really existed."

I just looked at him with wide eyes.

"It's not that I've replaced her with you, Lex, you've just helped me to see that there's more out there for me than what I thought there was."

My heart soared at his confession.

Is he talking about me?

"But where does that leave us when I go back home?" I asked quietly.

"I'm not sure," he admitted. "But we'll figure that out when the time comes," he promised.

I've never been very good at leaving things to the unknown.

"But seriously, Colt, I think we both know it's going to hurt... and I've accepted that, it's worth it to spend the time with you." I sighed. "I just can't figure out a way to avoid it."

"I'm scared too," he replied quietly. "Let's just give it some time," he suggested. "See how these few days go, and then we can talk about it. But I think it's pretty safe to assume I'm open to almost anything when it comes to you, Lexie."

I fiddled with the zip on my jacket.

He was right. There was no point in getting ahead of ourselves – worrying about things that might not even matter.

"Okay," I agreed. "I can live with that."

He reached for my hand and pulled it up to his lips, placing a chaste kiss on my knuckles.

"Colt?" I asked, as he drove us through the quiet streets.

"Yeah?" he answered, squeezing my hand at the same moment.

"Do you think it's too weird... that you've, you know... *slept* with one of my best friends?"

It was a question I thought I should ask him too. I'd asked Quinn, but Colt and I hadn't spoken about it since the first night at his club. It wasn't that it bothered me, even though it probably should have... and it wasn't as though I actively thought about it; I seemed to be able to ignore it as though it had never really happened. Even so, it needed to be discussed.

The thought of Colt with anyone but me made me feel surprisingly jealous, but no more so because it was Quinn than it would if it were any other woman.

He was quiet for a moment, obviously thinking through his answer.

"You know what I think?" he finally said.

"What?" I replied quietly, feeling slightly worried about what he might say.

"I think that it was meant to be like this."

His response shocked me, but I didn't get a chance to reply before he carried on.

"Sure, it might have been easier If Quinn had just met Harrison before she'd met me, and if I had met you before I'd met her... but that's not the way life works sometimes."

He paused for a moment, thinking it through.

"I think it's all just stepping stones. I was Quinn's stepping stone on her way to finding Harrison... and she was my stepping stone on my way to finding you."

His words gave me tingles.

He laughed lightly. "Maybe I'm just a sap." He shrugged. "But I like to think that everything happens for a reason."

I was so far gone over this man, I couldn't even think of a reply.

14. Colt

"Remind me how the hell we forgot this bloody thing again?" I called out as I entered my apartment with the morning-after pill I'd just retrieved from my car.

The truth was, I knew *exactly* how we'd forgotten.

After leaving Harrison's, I'd attempted to drive us around town, to show Lexie some of the sights. I'd even suggested another driving lesson, but it was a total waste of time. We only had eyes for each other. It was a struggle to even keep my eyes on the road with her sitting right next to me, giving me seductive looks.

I'd pulled the pin on the tour and the minute we'd parked in the underground parking area of my building, Lex was on me. I didn't know when she'd unbuckled, but the second I had the key out of the ignition she'd been right there in my lap, her gaze hot and urgent.

It had taken every inch of my self-control to not take her right there and then, but it was a public garage and exhibitionism wasn't exactly my thing. In fact, the thought of someone seeing Lexie like that made my blood boil.

The morning-after pill was long forgotten as we'd hurried upstairs and spent the rest of the night naked, tangled up in one another.

Lexie made me forget *everything*.

"Well I don't know about you... but *my* mind was on other things." Lex purred as she strolled out into the living room wearing nothing but my shirt. She'd claimed it as her own on her first night and I didn't have any intentions of ever getting it back.

My t-shirts have officially become our *t-shirts.*

She shot me a suggestive smirk as she approached.

I swallowed deeply, my throat suddenly dry. There was just something about this woman. She had this aura of innocence – a kind of purity about her, but she was sexy as sin at the same time.

She drove me wild with desire. It didn't seem to matter how many times I had her, it was never enough – last night was testament to that, because even though we'd been at it half the night, here I was, getting hard again at the very sight of her.

"You're a terrible influence." I groaned as she pressed her tight little body up against mine. She was bare under my shirt and it wasn't helping me focus.

"Who, me?" she teased with a sexy pout.

My eyes traced the curve of her lips as her tongue darted out to moisten them.

Shit.

She bit down on her bottom lip and my mind turned to mush.

"Food," I mumbled. "Energy," I blurted out.

What the hell am I trying to say?

Lexie giggled. "Are you hungry, babe?"

I'm hungry alright. But not just for food…

My stomach growled in protest of my thoughts. My body needed fuel. We'd forgotten to eat last night entirely – that's how we'd missed the pill.

Lex giggled again. "Food it is. I gotta take care of my man now, don't I?"

She turned and breezed into the kitchen, her sexy legs on full display.

I stood stock still, gawking like a fool at the woman who was slowly making me question every single priority I had.

Right now, all I saw was her.

I'd be her man every damn day of the week.

***

"Do you need to rest or something now?" I asked her with poorly concealed concern lacing my voice.

She'd finally taken the morning-after pill, and I had to admit, there was a tiny pang of sadness watching it go down.

A baby in her belly would have ensured this woman would be in my life forever.

Dial down the crazy, man; dial that shit riiiiggghhhtt down…

It's done now and it's for the best.

I was worried about how the medication might make her feel. I'd searched online for the side effects while she was in the pharmacy yesterday, and I didn't like what I saw.

Headaches, nausea, vomiting, cramps, dizziness...

My palms started sweating at the thought of her being unwell. I rubbed them on my jeans and tried to stay calm. The last thing she needed on top of all of that crap was stress.

"I'm *fine*," she reassured me.

I frowned at her and opened my mouth to spurt off the side effects I'd already informed her of.

"I know, Dr. Google, I know I *might* get sick, but right now, I'm fine. So, let's go do something fun." She pushed her chair back and it made that awful scraping noise against the flooring.

I shuddered.

She scooped up our plates and giggled at my grimace.

We'd fallen into an easy habit where one of us would cook and the other would clean up after. Although most of the time we both found ourselves in the kitchen watching the other one work, as neither of us really wanted to be too far away from each other.

"You really hate that noise don't you?" she mused.

I leaned back and threw an arm over the back of my chair, watching her every movement with a fascination that went way beyond a man watching a woman doing the dishes. "Doesn't everyone?"

"I dunno." She shrugged. "But I like knowing that you hate it."

I chuckled. "You some kind of sadist, Lexie Chase?"

She slid the plates into the dishwasher and her sweet laughter rang out through the room. "I meant so I could avoid doing it, you nut bar. I like learning about what you like and dislike." She shrugged and loaded some of the ingredients we'd used to make the omelets back into the fridge. "And not so that I can punish you," she added with a giggle.

"Good to know," I drawled, a smirk on my face. I knew what she meant. I got a little thrill every time I learned something new about her too. I loved knowing that she put her socks and shoes on, sock, shoe, sock, shoe, rather than sock, sock, shoe, shoe like I did.

It was the stupid little nothings that meant the most.

She bent down and my shirt rose up even higher on her thighs, revealing the bottom of her butt cheeks.

I groaned.

This woman was literally trying to kill me.

"I think you should put some pants on," I suggested, my eyes glued firmly to the curve of her ass.

"And why is that?" She smirked, clearly enjoying teasing me.

"Because you need another driving lesson, and if you stay here looking like that, we'll never make it out of this apartment."

She stood up straight and the shirt dropped lower, covering her again. She had a devious smirk in her eye. She wandered over towards the doorway, knowing full well that my attention was entirely on her.

"Are you sure that's what you want to do?" she asked as she turned and leaned against the door fame, her eyebrow raised and her pose sexy as hell.

God, I wanted her so badly, but my body needed a break. It felt like I'd had more sex in the past few days than I'd ever had in my entire life.

She laughed lightly, apparently able to read my thoughts now and shrugged. "Oh well, there's always later."

She swayed her hips down the hall, and I nearly fell off my chair leaning out to watch her.

Oh hell yes, later it is.

15. Lexie

"Seriously, woman, not so heavy on the gas," Colt hissed as he braced his hands on the dashboard.

"Sorry!" I squeaked.

I tried to press more lightly on the pedal this time, but the car still lurched forwards again.

Fail.

I slammed my foot down on the brake and nearly gave us both whip-lash as it came to a screaming halt.

I grimaced as I turned slowly to look at the only man that had ever been brave enough to get into a car with me twice.

Colt took a deep breath and released the death grip he had on the handle of the door.

"I really thought you'd be better this time." His words sounded like an apology.

I stared at him before bursting out laughing. "I'm sorry," I choked out between giggles. "I'm so terrible."

He'd joined me laughing. "I'm sorry, babe, but you really are the worst." He shook his head. "I don't think you're teachable."

"I tried to tell you," I insisted, wiping the tears of laughter from the corners of my eyes. "My dad swore he was never getting in the car with me ever again after the first time, I nearly wrapped us around a lamp post."

"Maybe I should consider myself lucky then." He winced.

"Maybe you should do the driving from now on?"

"It pains me to give up on you like this, but I think that might be wise."

"Consider it self-preservation." I snickered.

He barked out a laugh. "Let's go do something that won't get us both killed."

***

"There is no way I'm spending precious time with you, shopping."

"Please?" I pouted, giving him the puppy-dog eyes I knew he couldn't resist.

"What's wrong with my apartment?" he grumbled.

"There's nothing wrong with it," I cooed, like I was talking to a small child. "It just needs a few touches."

"What kind of touches?" he huffed as he let me drag him into the homeware section of the store.

"Some throw rugs, maybe a few cushions." I pointed out some things on display, but didn't stop. "Ooooh what about a print for the wall?"

He groaned and tugged me back against his body. "I'm not feeling tired anymore." He ground his hips against mine suggestively in what he must have known was a futile attempt to get out of the store.

I just laughed and kissed his lips. "Cute, babe, but you're not getting out of it that easy." I peeled his hands off my hips and tugged him along behind me again. "C'mon, we'll have the bachelor pad feel slapped right out of that place in no time."

***

Colt was now the proud new owner of several cushions, two throws, a floor rug, some framed prints and a variety of pointless knick-knacks that he'd shaken his head at. I'd even managed to convince him to buy a new cover for the duvet on his bed, complete with matching pillows.

He'd grumbled and groaned about eighty percent of the time, but I think, secretly, he had actually enjoyed himself. He certainly seemed more than happy with the finished product.

"It *does* feel more like a home now," he mused as he looked around the room.

"See? I told you it would make a difference," I boasted from my spot on the couch.

"It's not the cushions." He laughed lightly. "It's you." His expression turned serious. "*You* make this place a home."

My breath caught in my throat. I couldn't handle it when he talked like that. He had this unique ability to turn my insides to jelly.

I knew I was blushing, *again*. I don't think I'd blushed as much in my entire life as I had these past few days with him. He made me feel things no one else ever had, and I doubted ever would.

"You make me feel like I'm home," I replied in a whisper.

He didn't say another word. He sauntered towards me, sexy as anything I'd ever seen, and lifted me clear off the couch and into his arms.

I clamped my legs around his waist and looked right into his golden eyes that were full of heat and passion.

He walked us down the hall and into his bedroom, kicking the door shut as he went. I could feel the pull of his strong muscles under my hands and god, it felt so good.

There was no better place to be than in Colt's arms, he made me feel so safe and protected, like nothing bad would ever happen to me while he was around.

He turned and sat himself on the edge of his bed, so I was in his lap, straddling him. The look in his eyes was so tender... so loving. I could have spent all day looking into those eyes.

There was something else in there too, right now he was worried. I could see that he was waging a battle within his mind about us, about what would happen... what we would do after this magical time together was over.

I knew, because I was facing the same thing in my own head.

I can't do this right now.

"Lexie, I need..."

"Shhh," I cut him off, placing a finger softly to his lips.

He looked at me in question.

"Right now, I just need *you*," I whispered. "Please," I begged. "Just let us have this moment."

He nodded and tugged me in closer before his lips met mine.

16. Colt

Shit, shit, SHIT.

I wasn't entirely sure how I'd managed to get myself in this situation. The only explanation I had was that Lexie had me so distracted I'd forgotten about the life I had before she arrived.

Shiiiiitttt!

The message on my voicemail began playing again.

Gabby...

I don't know how the hell I had forgotten about my date with Gabby tonight. But I knew one thing; there was no way in hell I was going on that date now.

The only date I'll be going on is with Lexie.

"Call me back, handsome, I can't wait to see you tonight." Her grating voice played aloud in the room, the sound like nails on a chalkboard.

How had I ever found her attractive?

I turned around, phone in hand, ready to call her back and cancel our plans, when my eyes landed on Lexie.

She was standing in the doorway, and the look on her face and the hurt in her eyes assured me that she'd heard the entire message.

Oh no...

"Shit, Lex, it's not what—"

"It's all good," she interrupted me quickly, holding up her hands. "I get it, Colt, you had a life here before I came along and you'll still have one after I'm gone." She took a couple of steps back. "It's all good," she repeated quietly.

"Lex, I—"

She cut me off before I could tell her that I was one hundred percent cancelling this date. Just the thought of it made me feel sick.

"Quinn just called anyway, I'm gonna head over there. She's got an early finish." She backed up a little further.

I knew what she was doing. She was putting her walls up to protect herself.

The days we had together were passing by faster than I would have ever thought possible. We were on limited time and neither of us knew what would happen when that time ran out. I knew we needed to talk about it, I'd tried earlier, but it wasn't the right time. Now apparently wasn't the right time either, Lexie looked like she wanted to bolt.

Is she looking for a clean break now?

I didn't think she wanted out, not really. Yes, she was obviously scared, but she knew we had something special between us... she *had* to know that like I did.

"Lexie, I'm not going on that date." I took a step towards her, and she took another back away from me.

"You should," she encouraged.

I knew she didn't mean it. Her eyes were so full of hurt, she looked like she was on the verge of tears, but that didn't stop her words from cutting like a bitch.

I froze. "You want me to go on a date with another woman?" I asked in disbelief, my voice breaking.

She nodded at the same time as her eyes screamed no. "Sure, why not? I'll be gone on Friday anyway."

I rubbed my hand over my chest where an ache was forming. "Lexie..."

"It's fine," she mumbled as she turned and disappeared from sight.

I couldn't seem to make myself follow her; it was like the shock of the situation had glued me to the spot.

I heard her fumbling around in the living room, the sound of the door opening and closing, and then only silence.

She was gone.

17. Lexie

God damn word vomit.

I hadn't meant a single word I'd said back there. But they just kept coming out. Absolute nonsense had spilled from my mouth and I couldn't seem to find a way to stop it.

I didn't want Colt going on a date with another woman... just the thought of it made me want to hurl.

But I'd told him to do it.

What the hell is my deal?

My story about Quinn having an early finish had been complete bullshit, but I had nowhere else to go.

So here I was, sitting on Harrison's couch, crying like a fool. The poor cab driver that had had the misfortune of pulling over for me had dropped me off here about half an hour ago and retreated out that driveway as fast as he could. It was almost comical really; the effect a crying female could have on a man.

I'd half expected Colt to have turned up looking for me by now, but he hadn't. And even though I didn't deserve to be chased, I was still holding onto hope that this wasn't the end of us. I wanted him to come for me, even though it should have been me going back to him.

"Quinn?" a deep voice called from the direction of the garage.

Oh no...

This might have been Harrison's house, but I was not prepared for him to arrive home at four in the afternoon. I thought I'd have at least another two hours to get myself together and get my story straight before either of them walked through the door and caught me hiding out here.

"Quinn?" he called again.

"It's Lexie," I called back, wiping away my tears and doing my best to keep the emotion out of my voice.

Pull yourself together.

"Lexie?" he asked, confusion thick in his tone. "What are you doing here?" He appeared in the doorway to my left and I kept my eyes down. The last thing I needed was him seeing how bloodshot they were from crying.

"I thought I'd spend the night with you guys... if that's okay?" I sniffed.

"Lexie?" he asked quietly, his voice full of concern. "You're crying... what's wrong?"

"I'm fine," I answered as I stood up, my eyes still firmly on my feet.

"Lexie you're not—"

"Really, I'm fine, fine, fine," I rambled, cutting him off. "I might just go take a shower, you know, freshen up." I escaped the room as fast as I could before he could ask me anything more.

"Okay?" He said it like a question. "Well, you know you're always welcome here," he called after me.

I nodded to acknowledge I'd heard him and made my way quickly up the stairs to the safety of the bathroom.

I knew his eyes were on my back the whole time.

18. Colt

"What'd you do this time, bone head?"

I closed my eyes and braced myself for the wrath of my oldest brother. Harrison had obviously heard from Lexie, or more likely, Quinn had heard from Lexie and now Harrison was being sent to give me my warnings.

"Is she at your place?" I asked as I put on my turn signal and pulled over. "And did you really just call me a bone head?"

She wasn't answering her phone and I was starting to get worried. I'd driven around a few of the places I'd shown her, that she'd loved, but she wasn't at any of them. There weren't that many places I thought she would have gone, and Harrison's was the next stop on my list.

"That depends what you did to her," he answered, ignoring my question about his five-year-old name calling.

"Is she with Quinn?"

"No," he answered curtly. "Skippy's in meetings all afternoon."

"*You've* seen Lexie?" I asked, my shock evident.

"That depends what you did to her," he repeated.

He's with Lex...

I was surprised at that. Lexie was a private and proud girl. She wouldn't have liked Harrison seeing her in a vulnerable position. If I had to guess, I would say she was expecting to be at the house alone.

"It was just a misunderstanding," I mumbled.

"What did you do?" he asked again.

I ran my free hand over my face in frustration.

"This chick, Gabby, left me a voicemail about our date tonight." I sighed. "I'd forgotten all about it. Lex heard."

"Okay... dick move, but you cancel... problem solved."

Like I didn't think of that, jackass.

"I tried to tell her that I wasn't going to go. I mean, fuck, man, I organized it before I'd ever even heard the name, Lexie Chase. It's hardly *my* fault."

"Just get to the part where she ends up crying on my couch," he demanded.

Shit.

The thought of her crying hurt me deep in my chest.

"She told me I should go on the date. Spilled some crap about me having a life before her and needing to have one after."

"And you believed her? Dude, do you even know one single thing about women?"

"I didn't say I was going to go," I growled.

"Did you make sure she knew you *weren't* going to go?"

"I told her... but I didn't follow her and make *sure* she knew..." I groaned. "But she's the one who told me I should go, how is this *my* fault?" I rubbed my temple. This mess was giving me a headache.

"It's always your fault, man. The sooner you accept that, the better."

"You're a jerk."

"Just get your shit together, Colt, crying females make me nervous."

"Is she okay?" I asked quietly.

"She's fine, fine, fine. Her words, not mine."

I huffed out a laugh.

I may have been screwing this up, but contrary to my brother's belief I *did* know one thing, when a woman said she was fine, she most certainly was *not* fine.

"Shit," I mumbled.

"Shit indeed," he agreed.

"I need your help."

"Of course you do," he replied smugly.

***

I glanced at my reflection in the mirror and straightened my bow tie for what must have been the millionth time. I still didn't know if this was a good idea or not. I was still confused about what Lexie wanted, but I had to hope that I was doing right by her.

I ran my hand through my hair again. This was about as good as it was going to get.

I sighed at my reflection and turned to leave the room.

I had a feeling that my decision with this date tonight was going to be the most important one of my life so far.

"Falling for him wasn't falling at all. It was walking into a house and suddenly knowing you were home."

\- r.i.d.

19. Lexie

"I can't go out, Q; all of my stuff is at Colt's place," I whined in what I knew was a futile attempt to change her mind. Quinn never changed her mind unless she wanted to.

"Well then we'll just go around there and get something for you to wear to dinner," she suggested. "Problem solved."

"I don't really want to do that," I admitted sheepishly.

The idea of seeing Colt made my stomach churn with nerves.

"I'll call him," she insisted. "I'll tell him to take a walk for half an hour and you can have the place to yourself."

I knew she wasn't even joking.

Only Quinn could ring her ex and order him around.

I rolled my eyes. This whole thing was so stupid it was making my head hurt. Going back there would be like a burglar returning to the scene of the crime.

I just wanted a quiet night in to think about what an idiot I was, but no one ever won an argument against Quinn, and I was no exception.

"Fine." I admitted defeat. We both knew I was going to give in eventually, so I figured I may as well get on with it.

Quinn clapped her hands together in glee.

Ugh.

***

A funny feeling settled in my stomach as Quinn opened the door to Colt's apartment. I was so nervous. It didn't seem right being here without him, and I was beginning to wish that I could take back Quinn's request for him to take a walk.

I wanted to see him, to apologize and beg him to give me another shot at whatever this was that we had going on.

I desperately hoped that he wasn't out on his date with that heinous-sounding girl on the phone.

What the hell was I thinking?

Telling him that he should go out with that woman was probably the single most stupidest thing I'd ever done.

"Go get changed." Quinn ushered me further into the apartment. She'd already done my hair and makeup back at Harrison's house. I wasn't sure why I needed to get so dressed up for a dinner out with the two of them, but I just didn't have the energy to argue with her anymore.

Life is easier when Quinn gets her way.

I trudged my way down the hallway and paused before I entered Colt's room.

This doesn't feel right.

I glanced at the bed as I walked in, and was hit with a visual of all the intimate times we'd had together on that bed already.

This is your own fault.

I took a deep breath and decided to just get on with it. I could have my meltdown in the privacy of my own bed tonight, not here, where Quinn would be coming to find me if I took longer than a few minutes.

I heard the phone ring as I fastened the zip on the side of my favorite navy blue cocktail dress. I pulled out my tan heels to pair with it and I slipped one on as the answering machine clicked on and Colt's voice filled the apartment.

I sighed and my eyes burned with unshed tears at the already achingly familiar sound of his voice.

"You missed me, leave a message after the…"

The beep sounded.

"Hi there, I'm calling for a Mr. Colton Hunt, confirming your eight o'clock reservation for two at The Water House. We will see you tonight, sir." A chipper-sounding woman spoke.

My stomach dropped.

He's going on his date.

I'd really done it. It was all ruined.

I glanced around the room, and felt totally lost. I knew I should probably have packed up all my stuff, but all I wanted to do now was curl up in a ball and cry.

What if he brings her back here?

The thought made me sick to my stomach, but I decided that if he was going to bring another woman back here, he would be doing it with all of my crap surrounding him. I grabbed my small evening bag off the bed and slung it over my shoulder.

I needed to get the hell out of here – now.

"Quinn?" I called down the hall. "I want to go home."

I got no reply.

"Quinn?" I called again. "Please? I can't do this right now."

"You're not going anywhere, little bird."

My head snapped up at the sound of his voice.

Colt.

There he was, standing in the living room, dressed in a tuxedo.

My step faltered and I felt weak at the knees. He looked magnificent.

"God, you look beautiful, Lexie," he breathed, taking his fill of me from across the room. "Perfect."

My lip quivered under his intense stare.

"Except for those sad eyes." He whispered the words like an apology.

I didn't know what to say, or what to do. I was frozen to the spot.

"I don't understand," I finally managed to choke out. "Shouldn't you be on your date?"

His golden eyes turned soft as he shook his head. "The only person I'll be taking on a date is you, Lex. I don't care if you tell me to see other women. The only one I see is you."

What was I thinking?

Goosebumps prickled my skin. "I didn't mean it," I blurted out. "I'm so sorry, I didn't mean it." I felt a tear slip from the corner of my eye.

"Oh, Lex." He sighed, holding his arms open, welcoming me. "I know you didn't."

I rushed towards him and he enveloped me in his strong grip, holding me tight and safe. The addictive scent that could only be his enveloped me and I was home.

"I shouldn't have let you leave," he apologized.

"I shouldn't have gone," I sobbed.

"Shhhh," he cooed, trying to soothe me.

"I'm scared," I admitted once I was able to pull myself together enough to form coherent thoughts.

"What are you scared of, babe?" he asked softly, rubbing gentle circles on my back.

I wasn't one hundred percent sure now, it was a lot less scary when I was here, safe in his arms.

"I'm scared of losing you," I replied, my voice cracking at the end.

"Oh, Lexie." He sighed. "I'm scared too."

"You are?" I peeked up at him.

He looked down, right into my eyes. "I'm *terrified*." He brought his hands up to cup my face. "I think I'm starting to fall in love with you, Lex, and I'm terrified that I won't get to keep you."

My heart sped up into overdrive. Hearing that this man was falling in love with me, was like no other feeling in the world.

I'm falling for you...

"I want to keep you too," I whispered.

Forever.

"I've never felt this way about anyone before you, and it's scaring the hell out of me," I confessed, deciding to put my feelings out there.

His answering smile was dazzling. He was so beautiful when he smiled.

"We'll figure it out together, little bird, just you and me." He ran his hand through the long strands of my hair. "Just no more running, okay?"

"No more running," I promised.

***

"I feel kind of bad for ditching Q and Harrison," I admitted sheepishly as Colt held out the chair and gestured for me to sit down.

Such a gentleman.

He took his seat opposite me and flashed me his best megawatt smile, the one that took my breath away. "Don't sweat it; they were both in on the plan. And we'll meet back up with them later; I have another surprise for you."

Sneaky.

"There's more than this?" I gestured to the grand room around us. The Water House was the most beautiful restaurant I'd ever set foot in. I blushed a little with embarrassment at my own stupidity, having assumed earlier that this was where Colt was going to bring that other woman he'd promised his time to.

Stupid.

I took a deep breath and looked around the amazing restaurant he'd brought me to. The view of the water was out of this world. The whole place had a magical feel to it. I don't know whether that was more to do with the company I was keeping, or the aesthetics, but either way, I was entirely captivated.

"I can't guarantee it'll be this pretty, and we'll be well and truly overdressed, but it'll be fun." He winked.

"I like fun," I reassured him.

He smiled at me and I could tell he was truly happy, sitting here across from me.

I took a moment to appreciate again, just how fine he looked in his tux. It was a sight to behold, that was for damn sure.

"You should wear one of those every day," I told him with a sigh when he noticed my roaming eyes.

He raised his brows. "This monkey suit does it for you, huh?"

I fanned my face dramatically. "Oh, you have *no* idea."

He smirked, his eyes devious and filled with promise. "Oh I think I have a pretty good idea, Lex, if that blush on your cheeks and the way you keep shimmying in your seat are anything to go by."

I heard myself gasp.

"You can't even see what's in my seat."

He shrugged. "So you didn't just rub those sexy thighs together?"

Caught red-handed.

I scowled at him, trying to refrain from smiling and giving myself away. "*Maybe* I did."

He leaned across the table towards me and I instinctively leaned forward to meet him halfway.

"Don't forget, sweet little Lexie, that I know *exactly* how you look when you come, I know how you look when you're close and I *definitely* know how you look when you're in the mood."

His breath was warm at my ear and his close proximity gave me a fresh wave of goosebumps.

My heart thumped in my chest, and I knew that it wouldn't take much more than a whispered word and promise of a private spot from this man and I'd be there, ready and willing.

I was hit with a visual of the two of us inside a dark janitor's closet, my dress pushed up around my hips and Colt pounding into me, his black slacks still around his ankles.

Colt chuckled and leaned back in his chair, disrupting my little fantasy.

"I think I'd really enjoy whatever it was that was going through your head just now." He grinned.

I scowled at him, but I couldn't keep it up for long before a smile broke through. "Behave yourself, and I might show you some time."

***

"Well I officially feel sick," Colt announced, sitting his hands on his still flat belly as though he was all of a sudden the size of a house.

"I think that second piece of mud cake might have done it," I offered helpfully.

"I regret nothing."

I giggled and just looked at him. He was so handsome. I felt like the luckiest girl in this restaurant... this town... hell, this whole country.

He's here with me.

It was obvious he felt the same way about me, even if I did feel so full I was worried about splitting my dress, he still looked at me like I hung the moon.

Colt wasn't one of those guys who felt the need to hide his feelings, or put on some type of macho show. He wasn't the 'tough guy' type. He was sweet and genuine and if he felt something, he made sure you knew he thought you were special.

It was a rare quality to find in a man these days; the world was filled with so much bullshit and deception.

But not Colt.

He was here, he was happy, and so was I.

"Can I ask you something?" I questioned shyly.

I wasn't sure why I was asking this, but I just had the desire to know.

His lip twitched with amusement. "You want to know what I told my date, don't you?"

I narrowed my eyes at him. "That was a lucky guess."

He chuckled and I stared at him, waiting politely for him to answer me.

"What are you hoping I told her?" He asked coyly.

"Oh no." I shook my finger at him. "That's not how this works... no tricking me into giving you the answers. I want to know what really happened."

He looked at me for a few beats and I could tell he was weighing up whether or not to give me the smartass answer, or the real one.

"I called her," he finally said. "And I told her that I was sorry, but I wouldn't be going out with her or anyone else."

I let out a relieved breath.

"Then I told her that I'd met the most incredible woman, and that I couldn't see myself ever getting over her, so she should delete my number," he added simply, like he hadn't just said one of the most incredible things a man had ever said to me.

I swallowed the lump in my throat. "You said that?"

"I did. She wasn't even mad. She said she thought I was very sweet and wished us luck."

"*Really*?" I asked in surprise. I'm not sure I would have been that mature about getting the flick on the day of a date.

He laughed and shook his head. "Nah, not really. She called me an asshole and hung up on me."

That sounds more like it.

I giggled and winked at him. "You're *my* asshole though."

20. Colt

Sitting across the table from this woman, and not being able to put my hands on her was a tough gig.

If she giggled like that, or flipped her hair one more time, I swear to God I was going to lose my mind.

I'd instantly regretted not taking her someplace with a cozy, private booth in the back corner, but Lexie deserved to be spoiled. The Water House had the best food in the whole city, and if it weren't for the fact that a good friend of mine was the head chef, we wouldn't have had a shot in hell at getting a table without at least two months' notice.

She took a sip from her glass of wine and damn it all to hell, even watching her swallow was getting me hard.

I'd nearly lost my mind earlier when I'd watched her get lost in her own head. I knew what direction her thoughts had taken. Her eyes were smoldering and she was biting down on her bottom lip – a clear tell that she was thinking dirty thoughts.

Maybe we should go straight home after all...

"Did I tell you how beautiful you look tonight?" I asked her as my eyes trailed over her tanned shoulder and down her bare arm.

"You did." She smirked.

I'd told her at least fifteen times in the past two hours.

"You look perfect."

She shook her head in disagreement. "*Nobody* is perfect."

I studied her blue eyes and I couldn't think of anything that had ever looked that beautiful. Her sweet smile was so stunning; it warmed every inch of my insides when I was on the receiving end of one of her smiles.

She is perfect.

"You're perfect in my eyes," I offered.

And that's all that matters.

I heard her sigh and look at me in that dreamy way she did that I still wasn't used to.

I didn't know why Lexie was so surprised by me thinking the world of her. Lawson treated Ellerslie like the entire universe revolved around her, he worshipped the ground that woman walked on. And Harrison, even though he seemed to have missed out on the romance gene, still showed in everything he did, just how much he loved Quinn.

Her friends were surrounded by love, and so was she... she just didn't know it yet.

***

I gave Cam a salute as I walked Lex towards the front door, my hand resting on the small of her back.

Cam grinned his smartass grin and made a humping motion with his hips, gesturing to Lexie.

I held back a laugh.

He's such a douche-bag sometimes.

He'd come over to our table earlier and done his best impression of the charming chef, flirted his ass off with my girl and tried to goad me any chance he got. I loved him to death, but that guy could be a total pain in my ass.

Lexie must have caught sight of Cam taking the piss, because she flipped him the bird, a playful smile on her face.

He pretended to catch it and slip it into his pocket.

I couldn't help but laugh at that.

"Sorry about him." I held Lexie's coat out for her and she slipped into it.

She giggled. "Oh, don't be... he's harmless."

She turned to face me. "So, what now?" She asked excitedly as we strolled outside hand-in-hand and I flagged down a cab.

"It's a surprise." I tapped the end of her nose as she pouted.

Lexie apparently didn't do well with surprises; she'd been on my case ever since I told her I had something fun planned. I loved learning things like that about her. It was something that was probably going to drive her mad if we made this thing work long term, because I planned to spoil and surprise her any chance I got.

Lexie grumbled and turned her big blues onto me.

Those puppy eyes weren't going to work on me, not this time.

"Nope, that's not gonna work tonight." I chuckled and shook my head at her. "You'll just have to wait and see."

***

"Oh my god." She giggled as we walked in the door of the karaoke bar and she realized what we were here for.

I winced and mentally kicked myself for not finding out her thoughts about this kind of thing. "You think it's lame?" I asked, second guessing my idea.

"No way," she exclaimed, turning to face me. Her eyes were dancing with excitement. "I freakin' *love* karaoke!"

Phew...

I chuckled; she was almost bouncing with excitement. I loved seeing her so happy. I never imagined I could get this much joy out of making somebody else happy.

"One more surprise for you, babe." I placed my hands on her shoulders and turned her in the direction of where El, Quinn, Harrison and Lawson were sitting.

"Eeekkk," she cried, taking off towards them, towing me behind her. She stopped short, turned around and wrapped her arms around me, squeezing me tight. "Singing *and* my friends, I just might love you, Colton Hunt."

I swear my heart stopped in my chest.

I think I just might love you too.

I gave her a gentle nudge in the direction of her friends while I tried desperately to still my now erratically beating heart.

***

I couldn't help but laugh at the three of them up there; they were all glammed-up in beautiful dresses, perfect hair and makeup... and they were singing their own rendition of Vanilla Ice's 'Ice, Ice, Baby'.

It was fucking hilarious – without a doubt the funniest thing I'd witnessed in quite some time.

Half the bar was laughing at them, the other half were stopping just short of covering their ears.

Quinn and El couldn't rap to save their lives, Lex was slightly better, but even given that, the whole thing was still terrible to listen to.

Even Lexie can't save this performance.

"This is going on YouTube." Harrison sniggered. He was filming the whole thing on his phone.

Lawson had tears in his eyes from laughing so hard at his wife and younger sister.

Quinn was now doing her best impression of a gangster rapper, her hands flying all over the show in obscene gestures I'd never seen before.

I chuckled again as my eyes quickly found their way back to where they belonged.

My little song bird.

Lexie was having so much fun up there with her friends. Her cheeks were flushed and her eyes were bright. It was obvious that spending time with these girls was a happy place for her. I hadn't asked her much about the friends she had back home. I had met some of the girls she hung out with, back when I'd been seeing Quinn.

Brooke, Jemma and Stacey...

They'd come out to visit Q and El here, and we'd had a pretty crazy night. They were sweet girls, but a few drinks, combined with Lawson's mates and some type of stalker situation, and things had gotten out of hand fairly quickly.

I shook my head in amusement at that memory.

It was crazy to think that Lex was meant to have joined them on that trip.

I should have met her then.

And then there was El and Lawson's wedding celebration. Lexie hadn't been able to make it to that either... work had gotten in her way both times.

It was like fate hadn't been ready for us to meet just yet. I sent up a silent thank you to the karma gods, that I'd finally got my chance to meet her.

I'm going to miss her so much.

She was still rapping and her laughter rang out loud, pulling me from the sad hole I was falling into.

"Kill it, new girl," Harrison yelled.

That got a laugh out of me. Harrison, like the dickhead he was, had taken to calling Lexie 'new girl', presumably since he was under the impression I always had a new girl on the scene.

"She'll kick your ass if you keep calling her that," I warned him, half joking, half serious.

He laughed loudly. "She's the size of a grasshopper, man, what's she gonna do? Stomp on my foot?"

Valid point.

"And besides, she loves me really; she can't stay mad with her future brother in law for long," he taunted me, waggling his brows.

I wasn't giving him the satisfaction of a reaction. That, and I had no words – the idea of making Lexie mine forever, temporarily rendered me speechless.

I glanced around the room, looking for something, anything to distract me.

The girls had giggled their way off stage to a round of applause from the more amused group of patrons.

The microphone caught my eye.

My turn.

I strolled over to the song selections, leaving Harrison laughing after me.

I was going to sing a song for my girl. I took my time choosing, I wanted it to be as perfect as it could be, given that I would actually have to sing it.

I decided on Shawn Mendes' 'Kid in Love'.

I'd felt Lexie's eyes on me the entire time I'd been over here, but I couldn't look at her yet, I didn't want to risk losing my nerve.

It was time to show her exactly what was going on in my head, and in my heart. Lex had never heard me sing and I was nervous as hell. I wasn't great, but I wasn't terrible either.

I knew she wouldn't care how I sang; it was about so much more than the sound of my voice.

"That's your man, Lex!" I heard one of the girls cry out.

I approached the mic and waited for the cue on the screen to tell me to begin.

Here goes nothing...

I held back a grin as my eyes met Lexie's. I'd never seen a woman melt before, but I was pretty certain it would look something like the way Lexie was looking at me right now.

She was in full-blown swoon mode.

She sat her glass down and slowly made her way over to the front of the small stage.

Tingles raced up and down my spine.

I sang the song to her, like there was no one else around, and she stood there, a beautiful smile on her face as she absorbed my words. She grinned and surprised me by stepping up onto the platform and picking up the second mic.

She blew me a kiss before joining in.

We stood, facing one another, singing the words to each other.

Lexie may not have been able to make Quinn and El sound good, but she was certainly improving this song for me.

The beautiful harmony of her voice had everybody taking notice. It was hard to miss a voice like Lexie's. Suddenly the whole place was looking at us. I didn't care though – I was too busy looking at her.

I could hear Harrison and Lawson whooping and hollering as the song came to an end, and the whole joint erupted into applause.

Lexie turned and gave a curtsey, and I bowed, giving the small crowd a wave.

Lexie giggled as she looked up at me, and I could tell she was totally overwhelmed by my gesture.

I grabbed her and tucked her against me, placing a soft kiss to the top of her head as I led her down towards where our friends were waiting.

"I feel like I'm in a movie where the guy does sweet things for the girl," she gushed.

I chuckled, high-fiving Lawson as he made his way up for his own turn. He was a much better singer than I was, and he was bound to have his wife teary-eyed in no time, just like he had at their wedding.

"You are just full of surprises tonight." Lexie looked up at me, her eyes a little glassy. "Thank you for my song." She pushed up on her tippy toes, looking for a kiss.

I happily obliged, meeting her soft, sweet lips with a fervor I couldn't control.

She pulled back, and looked up at me with pure adoration in her eyes.

I love you.

I opened my mouth to tell her how I felt about her, but got interrupted by my pain-in-the-ass brother.

"Damn, new girl, I didn't think anyone could make this fool sound good up there."

Fucking Harrison.

Lexie did her best impression of shooting him daggers – a tough gig for such a sweet girl. "Call me that again and see what happens," she warned him.

I held back a laugh.

Harrison laughed loudly, but had the good sense not to push her any further. Lexie may have been small, but I wouldn't want to mess with her.

"Sorry he's such an ass, he just likes to try and wind me up... he knows you're my biggest weakness," I apologized on my brother's behalf as he disappeared to go and annoy someone else.

She laughed lightly and if I was reading her right, seemed a little chuffed at the idea of being my Achilles heel. "I don't actually care about the name; I just figure I should put him in his place before he gets any more silly ideas." She rolled her eyes.

"I knew you were a smart woman." I chuckled and placed a kiss on her forehead.

I wanted so badly to say those three little words to her, but I decided that maybe it was fate stepping in again... that maybe now wasn't the right time.

I did have a tendency to jump the gun and I didn't want to make that same mistake with Lexie. I hadn't even officially made her mine yet, and that was a situation that needed to be remedied.

Right now.

I tugged on her hand, drawing her attention back to me. "Can I talk to you about something?" I asked her, looking right into her beautiful bright blue eyes.

"Of course," she replied quickly. "You can always talk to me about anything," she promised.

"Well... I've been thinking a lot about... *us*..."

Her face dropped slightly.

"And I was thinking... I don't know what will happen from here, but I want to figure it out with you... as an official couple."

A huge, surprised grin broke out on her pretty face. "Are you asking me to be your girlfriend?"

I rubbed the back of my neck, embarrassed and nervous. "Uh... well, yeah... if that's something you might want to be..." I trailed off, feeling like I was twelve years old again and asking a girl out in the playground.

Shit.

"I would love to," she answered sweetly.

I couldn't contain the huge smile that spread across my face.

She's mine.

"You're not even going to give me grief about that botched up proposition?" I asked as I tugged her against my body.

She laughed and cuddled into me, filling my nose with the sexy perfume she always wore.

"I wouldn't dream of it," she promised.

Luckiest fool in this place.

***

"I know you don't dance, but pleeeeaaasse," Lex pleaded. "Just come and dance with me once. We can just sway."

I chuckled and took her outstretched hand. "What makes you think I don't dance?"

She frowned and narrowed her eyes at me. "Because you wouldn't dance with me at that charity event," she pointed out.

I smirked. "Oh, babe, that had a whole lot more to do with the tent I was pitching in my pants than it did with not being able to dance."

Truth was, I'd been hanging out to dance with her ever since. Having that tight little body grinding up against me...

Where do I sign?

This may not have been a hot and heavy night club like I would have liked, but it'd have to do.

Lexie's eyes dropped to my crotch and her jaw fell lax for a moment before she managed to get herself back together. "Hmm." She cleared her throat. "Okay... well... good."

I loved watching her eyes look at my body.

"So... is that, um, not so much of a problem now?" she asked curiously.

I pulled her in close and leaned down to whisper in her ear, my voice husky. "If you're asking is my dick hard, then, yes... it is." I pressed my hips against her belly to emphasize my point.

I'd been walking around in *at least* a half-hard state ever since I'd met her.

She let out a small gasp.

"But I don't need to hide it from you anymore, do I?"

She shook her head slowly and bit down on her lip.

God damn.

"Lead the way, little bird," I instructed.

***

We'd been home for ages, and Lexie had been asleep for a couple of hours now, but for some reason sleep still wouldn't take me. I'd been lying here, utterly mesmerized by the woman in my arms, to the point where I couldn't look away.

She was sleeping in my t-shirt, same as she had every other night, although she had a rotation of two or three different ones going now. I didn't care if she took every shirt I owned – they looked better on her anyway.

Her long, dark hair was swept back behind her, the silky strands tickling my arm whenever I moved. Her lips were parted slightly as she slept and her lashes twitched every now and then as she dreamed.

I would have given my left leg to know what went through that mind of hers while she slept so peacefully, but I never would. I'd have to settle for knowing that she thought about me during our time together, that much was obvious. There was so much joy in her eyes when she looked at me, and it made my heart soar. There was a hint of fear in there too, of what the future might hold, I assumed. But we were here, we were together and we could figure something out.

We had to.

I took a deep breath, absorbing the alluring scent that was entirely Lexie, and closed my eyes.

***

"Can I take you to meet some people today?" I asked Lexie shyly.

Nobody really knew what I got up to on a Tuesday. It was the one day of my week that I used to give back to the community I lived in. It was something I viewed as an important part of my life, but I kept it to myself. I'd never shared this with anyone.

She eyed me up, searching my face for clues as to why I might look so nervous.

"Why do you look weird? I've already met Harrison, it can't get much worse," she teased.

I laughed but still didn't answer as I rinsed my bowl out and put it into the dishwasher.

"Colt." Lexie's sweet voice caressed my name. "Tell me what's going on in that head of yours."

I rubbed at the back of my neck and turned to look at her, resting my hip against the kitchen countertop.

Her brilliant blue eyes were soft and welcoming. A sense of ease washed over me and I knew that I had found the right person to bring with me today.

"How about I show you instead?" I offered.

"Okay..." She nodded. "But you know I hate surprises, how am I meant to know what to wear?"

I looked her up and down. She had on blue jeans, a white long-sleeved t-shirt and socks.

"Go and chuck something warm on top and some shoes... then you'll be perfect," I instructed.

She gave me a salute and wandered off down the hall to do as I'd asked.

I wiped my hands down my jeans, my palms suddenly sweaty. I don't know why I was so nervous, but I guess that was the thing about opening up your life entirely to another person... you left yourself vulnerable.

Lexie appeared back in the kitchen, an excited smile on her face, dressed exactly as I'd suggested.

"Alright, let's do it." She winked.

Here goes nothing.

***

Lexie hadn't said a single word since we'd arrived at the retirement home. She'd eyed the sign curiously, but not asked a single question.

I'd opened her door for her, taken her hand in mine and led her through the big automatic doors at the front of the building.

I peeked down at her as we walked along the corridor in the direction of the main lounge. She was looking around, taking in the details and no doubt wondering why the hell I'd brought her here.

I glanced at my watch.

Ten o'clock. Perfect.

They would have just finished with morning tea.

I squeezed Lexie's hand as we walked into the big room.

"Oh, Colton," Betsy called from the armchair closest to the big window.

A huge smile broke out on my face. I could feel Lexie's eyes on me as I made a beeline for the older woman. I really tried hard not to have favorites, but I did have a particularly soft spot for Betsy.

"Hey, Bets, long time no see." I let go of Lexie and gave Betsy a gentle hug and a kiss on the cheek. She smiled brightly up at me from her chair and squeezed my hand.

I reached for Lexie's hand again and tugged her closer. "This is Lexie," I told Betsy. "This is my friend Betsy," I explained.

Lexie smiled. "It's nice to meet you."

"Oh God bless," Betsy cried. "Would you look at that, Susan, our Colton's brought his girlfriend along."

Susan looked up from her knitting. "Oh, well blow me down, so he has."

Lexie giggled next to me.

I groaned dramatically at their teasing. "Yes, everyone," I announced. "I have indeed brought my girlfriend with me today, her name is Lexie, and I want you all to be on your best behavior," I warned, my tone teasing.

They might have been a group of oldies, but they still had plenty of get up and go.

Lexie received a chorus of hellos and waves, which she graciously returned.

"That's Bob, June, Kate, Alfred, Elizabeth, Peter, Martin, Stuart, Susan, Shelley, Earl, Richard, Elle and Grace." I pointed out each of my friends to Lexie.

She looked up at me with an amused expression. "And which one are we here to visit?" she asked me in a hushed voice.

"All of them." I chuckled as she frowned.

She looked around the room. "Yeah... so... I'm confused," she admitted. "Are you related to everybody here?"

I laughed and kissed her forehead. "I'm not related to any of them."

"But you—"

"I come in every Tuesday and hang out for a few hours," I explained.

Her eyes widened in surprise.

"I sit with them, sometimes we just talk, they tell me stories from their younger days, or I might read for a bit... most of them haven't got much in the way of family around." I shrugged. "I dunno, they seem to enjoy it, and so do I."

Her eyes turned glassy as she looked at me. The expression on her face was one of total wonder. She pressed up on her tippy toes and kissed my jaw. "You are the most incredible man I have ever met in my entire life," she told me, absolute honesty in her eyes.

I swallowed deeply.

"So what are we doing today?" she asked, turning her attention back to Betsy.

My heart swelled in my chest.

I'm so glad I brought her here.

"Well, I don't know, dear, what do you think might be fun?" Betsy asked.

"Hmmmm..." Lexie thought about it for a moment. "When was the last time someone did your nails for you?" she asked.

Betsy smiled and her eyes lit up instantly. "About 1999, honey, so you can sign me up for that."

Lexie giggled, and for some reason the sound hit me like a wrecking ball right in the heart. That was the sound I wanted to hear, every day, for the rest of my life.

Just the fact that she was here, and with no prompting at all she was offering to do something nice for people I cared about... she really was amazing.

She was as close to perfect as a person could get.

"Count me in, angel," Kate called out to Lexie.

Lexie beamed back at her. "Brand spanking new nails for everyone." She winked.

***

I looked over at Lexie for what must have been the hundredth time, totally in awe of the beautiful woman beside me.

"What?" She giggled. "Why do you keep looking at me like that?"

I shook my head and ran my hand through my hair. "You were incredible today, you know that?"

She shrugged and blushed that pretty pink color I'd quickly grown to love. "It was fun… I didn't do anything special."

I chuckled.

She was down-playing the situation and we both knew it.

"Babe, not only did you paint every set of women's nails in that place, but you actually went out and bought the polish to do it."

Lexie had quickly discovered that the only nail polish available in the retirement village was a terrible shade of maroon. She'd declared that it wouldn't do, then she'd had me drive her to the closest pharmacy where she'd picked up at least eight different colors.

I'd never seen the ladies so excited.

Lexie had moved their chairs into a circle, with a small table in the middle and had set about her work. It was a sight that would have warmed even the coldest of hearts.

It was nothing special, just a couple of coats of color on their nails, but it was obvious that it meant so much more to these women.

The couple of hours I'd anticipated spending here had quickly turned into most of the day. I'd spent most of my time doing puzzles and reading with Bob, Richard and Earl, and watching football with Alfred and Peter. Martin had spent half of his time pointing out exactly how long it was going to take us to finish the puzzle, informing me that I had a terrible reading voice, and flirting with the ladies.

"You might not have thought it was a big deal, but the ladies certainly did, Lex. You talked with them, asked about their lives, you looked at pictures of their great grandchildren… what you did was more special than you probably realize."

Lexie blushed deeper.

"It breaks my heart that they don't get many visitors," I added.

She reached out and squeezed my hand. "They have you." Her voice and the look in her eyes told me that she believed that having me was more than enough.

"I know it doesn't make up for their families not being around, but it gives them something to look forward to," I agreed.

"I saw the way they all looked at you, Colt. You mean the world to those people."

Now it was my turn to blush.

"Thank you for letting me see that part of your life," Lexie said softly.

I looked over at her and knew that I'd undoubtedly made the right choice.

I knew in that very moment that *anything* involving sharing my life with Lexie was always going to be the right choice.

"I want a relationship where we can act like idiots, talk about the most random stuff, share music, and never get tired of each other."
-Author unknown

21. Lexie

"Hey, babe, I need to head out for a bit, do you want to come?" Colt called out to me before appearing in the doorway of the living room.

We'd ended up spending all day at the retirement home, rather than the few hours Colt had intended, and I'd just sat down on the couch while Colt had gone hunting through the kitchen to assess the options for dinner.

I glanced down at my heart-covered, flannel pajama bottoms and the black t-shirt of Colt's that I was currently wearing. My hair was all over the place; I'd just showered and washed it, but hadn't gotten around to brushing it yet. I wasn't even wearing a bra. I looked like a total mess.

I scrunched up my nose. "No luck with the food, huh?"

He shook his head. "Not a shot in hell of making a meal out of that." He gestured with his thumb over his shoulder in the direction of the kitchen.

"We could order in if you can't be bothered cooking tonight?" I suggested.

He shook his head "It's all good, I may as well get what we need for the next couple of days. You wanna come?"

I gestured to my attire. "I think I'll stay here."

He smirked. "Good call." He grabbed his keys off the side table. "Will you be okay here on your own?"

I rolled my eyes. "I'm not a baby in a hot car, Colt, I'll be fine," I reassured him.

There was no way I was going looking like this – that, and a new episode of Teen Wolf had just come on, so I wouldn't be moving far from this couch anyway.

He laughed his way to the door. "Tyler Posey has nothing on me, right, babe?"

"Not a thing on you," I promised with a wink.

It wasn't until after he'd left that I realized that he'd obviously been doing his research on my favorite show.

That man...

He is something special.

Looking around the room I realized I'd been living here for days, and neither one of us had done any cleaning. The sheets hadn't been changed, I had no idea how much laundry there was, and the kitchen needed a good once over. I decided I'd better give up my spot on the couch for now. I found the remote, hit record and went in search of the vacuum cleaner.

***

"Oh my god, they're so beautiful," I gushed as I accepted the enormous bunch of stunning flowers that Colt had returned with. "What on earth are they for?"

"Do I need a reason?" he asked over his shoulder with his eyebrow raised. He had begun unloading the groceries he'd just bought into the fridge.

"In my experience, albeit limited, men don't usually buy women flowers, *just because*," I explained.

"Then you haven't been spending time with the right man," he replied without missing a beat.

There is no doubt about that.

I just smiled stupidly at him, feeling like the luckiest woman in the world.

"And I got them because I had a feeling they would make you smile." He turned to face me. "Like you are right now... and I'm *never* going to need more of a reason than that, okay?" he told me, his tone gentle but insistent.

I nodded, the giant, goofy grin he was referring to, still firmly in place on my face.

"You're smiling like a loon." He chuckled.

I just nodded, still grinning.

"Here." He tossed me a small box of refills for my Polaroid camera.

"Oh my gosh." I swooned.

Just the fact that he knew the make and model of the camera I owned said volumes about how much attention he paid to me.

He laughed and shook his head in amusement at how content I was.

"Thank you," I told him quietly. "You certainly know how to make a girl feel special."

It wasn't even just the gifts, it was the way he looked at me... the way he constantly paid attention to my emotions... it was just *him*.

I'd never, ever, in my whole life, met someone quite like Colt.

"It's lucky I did buy them," he added as he looked around at the now considerably cleaner apartment. "This place looks amazing. You didn't have to do that."

"It no big deal," I insisted. "I've been living here too."

I fished around in the cupboard looking for a vase. I found a big glass jug and decided that it was probably the best I was going to find.

I could feel Colt's eyes on me as I sat the pink and white arrangement in the jug and placed them on the table.

"There." I smiled. "Now it's perfect."

"You won't get any argument from me," he replied, his voice deep and throaty as he wrapped his arms around me from behind.

I knew he wasn't talking about the flowers at all.

"I got something else too," he murmured in my ear.

"Oh yeah?" I asked, holding back a shiver from his closeness.

He reached around me into the one remaining bag left on the table, and when he pulled out series one, two and three of Teen Wolf on DVD, I couldn't help but laugh.

"You really are a sucker for punishment, huh?"

It was such a sweet, simple gesture. That was Colt down to a tee.

Sweet and uncomplicated.

"I thought I'd better check out my competition," he replied, and I could hear the grin in his voice.

I was fairly certain that there wasn't a man on the face of this earth that would be competition for Colton Hunt.

***

"Shit, Lex, I can't get anyone to cover for me." Colt slid in next to me on the couch, his face a mask of defeat.

I'd listened to him on the phone for the past half hour, calling employee after employee, trying to arrange for someone to take his manager's shift at the club this evening. He was having absolutely no luck.

I guess being the boss sucks sometimes.

"That's okay," I replied, trying my best to sound like I meant it. "I didn't expect you to take off work for me."

I truthfully didn't expect him to... but a girl could dream.

"You've only got two more nights here," he grumbled. "I don't want to waste one of them at work."

"It's fine," I reassured him. "I'll see what El is up to... she might want to go get dinner or catch a movie or something."

I knew it was pathetic, but I felt a huge sense of disappointment at the thought of having to be apart from him, even just for the night. I'd spent nearly every minute of my time with him these past few days, and I'd loved it. No matter how much time we spent together, I still wanted more.

We'd been here together all last night, and today, just doing nothing – but everything at the same time... and I still wasn't even a little bit sick of him.

"Or... you could come with me?" he suggested hopefully.

I scrunched up my nose. "I wouldn't get in the way?" I asked, just as hopeful that he'd tell me it was okay for me to tag along.

"Not even close," he assured me. "It might even be fun."

"Can I sit around and get drunk?" I bartered with him.

"I'm pretty sure my job requires me to ensure that people *aren't* getting drunk, but I could probably turn a blind eye, for a pretty little thing like you." He put on a southern drawl and winked at me.

"Well then, Mr. Bar Manager, you've got yourself a date."

***

I wasn't really one to frequent the club scene, but even I could tell that this place was on fire tonight.

I'd been expecting us to be heading up to the same V.I.P. area where we'd performed on Friday night, but instead, we were down on the main floor, and as the bar staff fondly referred to it, we were 'mingling with the civilians'.

I liked it better down here. There were more people, with fewer inhibitions for me to watch.

I was a rubbernecker from way back. That's what my mom always called me. Football games, concerts, movies... I found myself watching other people more than whatever it was my attention should have been focused on.

People tended to let loose when the lights went down – they let their usually more subdued personalities come out to play. A few drinks and a darkened room made for amazing people-watching. I'd just about seen it all in the past hour or so... some outrageous dance moves, hookups, fights, even some vomiting.

Right now, I was in a happy place. I was perched at the bar, where my hot-as-hell boyfriend – because I could call him that now, was mixing drinks like a pro, he had bottles flying in the air like some kind of ninja juggler and to say I was impressed would have been a total understatement.

Is it hot in here?

There was something about seeing him so in his element like this that just had me melting on the inside. It was like foreplay to me and all of a sudden I couldn't wait to get home and get him alone. I bit down on my lip and willed him to turn around and drag me away from here like some kind of caveman.

"What's a beautiful woman like you doing down here all alone?"

I groaned internally.

The one downside to sitting here all by myself was that I'd been hit on more times in the past two hours than I had in the past six years combined.

Apparently, sitting alone at a bar meant I had a giant neon sign flashing above my head that read 'available – hit on me'.

I grimaced as I turned to face my most recent admirer. A tall, dark-haired man with bronzed skin and brown eyes. If Colt had to watch me fend off yet another advance I was sure he was going to lose his mind.

I peeked over at the far side of the bar where Colt was thankfully busy entertaining a group of young patrons with his bottle acrobatic skills.

I cursed myself internally when I turned back and realized I'd given the stranger an opportunity to sit down next to me.

"I, ah... I'm not really interested, but thank you though," I offered politely.

"Thank you for what?" He chuckled.

My cheeks blazed. "Um... the compliment."

He laughed again and took a sip of the beer he was holding. "No problem."

He made absolutely no move to get up and leave me alone, and I grew more uncomfortable with each awkward second that passed.

"Get you a drink?" he suggested.

"What do you think?" I replied, indicating to my full drink.

Not interested.

This guy obviously couldn't take a hint.

"You know..." He smirked, noticing my rising agitation. "I'm surprised that he left you to fend for yourself... *anyone* could be coming on to you while he's busy with his circus tricks." He tsked. "I'll have to have a hard word with the little twerp."

I looked at him and gaped, then followed his line of sight to look at Colt, who was now looking in our direction and smirking back at the man next to me.

They know each other; looks like the joke's on me.

"That's not funny," I scolded the stranger. "You could have told me that you weren't just another random, I wouldn't have been such a bitch."

"And ruin all my fun?" He shook his head and laughed. "It's Lexie, right? I'm Angelo, Colton's cousin." He offered me his hand and I shook it.

The pieces clicked into place as I remembered Colt telling me about his cousin who worked for him at the club.

I turned towards him. "It's nice to meet you, Angelo, and I swear, I'm not usually such a hard ass."

He laughed and waved away my apology.

"I just seem to be getting a lot of unwanted attention tonight and I'm pretty sure Colt's had enough of it," I explained as I looked back at Colt, who seemed a bit more at ease now that I wasn't here all alone like a sitting duck.

He shot me a dazzling smile, momentarily taking my breath away, before turning back towards his work.

"Cue the helpful cousin." He pointed at himself.

The penny dropped.

"Ahhh." I nodded in acknowledgment. "He called in the reinforcements."

"He did."

I shook my head in amusement as I watched Colt work. "I'm sorry you got stuck with babysitting duty."

Angelo chuckled. "Hell, don't be sorry, if he wants to pay me to sit around and have a drink with a beautiful woman, then he can go right ahead."

I laughed. I had a feeling that Angelo and I were going to get along just fine.

"So, what have you been doing down here?" he asked. "Dancing?" He gestured towards the packed dance floor where the Justin Bieber remix of 'Despacito' was blasting.

I shook my head in amusement. "I wasn't brave enough to go in alone. I've just been admiring the eye candy." I tipped my head towards Colt. "And trying to decide if that guy over there is into the guy, the girl, or both," I mused as I pointed out the people I was referring to.

He nearly spat out a mouthful of beer. "You what?"

I laughed. It was probably weird to other people, but it was second nature to me.

"Yeah." I nodded enthusiastically. "Trying to figure out things about other people's lives is really fun, you should try it."

He tipped his head to the side as though he was attempting to figure me out. I took it as an opportunity to show him what I meant.

"Okay, so... see that blonde girl right there?" I pointed towards the dance floor at a girl who was out there shaking what her momma gave her.

He nodded. "I see her."

"Okay, so... I think she's something like a preschool teacher by day, but by night she lives out her real passion."

He chuckled. "And what's her real passion?"

"Erotic dancing," I answered. "And the guy in the checkered shirt?"

Angelo nodded again, seemingly amused by my little game. "He has a secret crush on her, he comes here every night, hoping she'll be here... and for the last thirty minutes he's been trying to figure out how to approach her without looking like he's just out for a piece of ass."

He laughed again. "You're a strange little thing."

"Don't knock it 'til you try it." I winked at him as I took a sip of the latest delicious concoction Colt had made for me. I'd only been joking when I'd told him I'd sit here and get drunk, but if he kept making me drinks this delicious, it wouldn't be long until I was on my ass; they were going down a bit too easy.

"Alright then, I'll give it a go," Angelo boasted, glancing around. "Okay... you see that couple over there, late thirties maybe?"

I followed the direction he was pointing. "I see them." I nodded.

"They're here for date night – they left the kids at home... two boys and a girl," he explained.

I giggled; thrilled that he was playing along.

"She's just told him she likes the idea of bringing another woman into the bedroom," he continued.

I laughed loudly.

"Obviously, he's ecstatic about the prospect... but he likes blondes and she'd rather a brunette, so they're having a hard time agreeing on who they should approach."

"You are far too good at this." I clutched my side; it was sore from laughing so hard at him.

"You were right, you know, this *is* fun," he admitted with a grin.

"Told you so."

The rest of the night passed with laughter, drinks and stolen kisses from Colt. I may have been sitting in a club with a near stranger for company, waiting for my boyfriend to finish work, but it was one of the most enjoyable nights I'd ever had.

And it's all because of him.

22. Colt

I let Callum know I'd be back behind the bar in ten minutes.

There was one thing I needed to do in this club tonight that had absolutely nothing to do with work, and everything to do with my girl grinding against me.

That little taste I'd gotten of dancing with Lexie at the karaoke bar had done nothing but add fuel to my fire. I wanted more. One time of anything was never going to be enough when it came to Lexie.

I need more.

I was getting her out on that packed dance floor, just like I should have done that very first night here.

I prowled towards the end of the bar where she was still perched, chatting with my cousin, Angelo.

They were laughing and joking and I gave myself a mental high-five for coming up with the idea of bringing him down here to look out for her. She was clearly enjoying the company, and as another bonus I could finally relax and do my job. I knew if I had to watch another drunk asshole hitting on my girl, I was going to hit the roof. Angelo had been the perfect solution.

Lexie saw me coming and smiled so big I was worried her face might break.

"Hey, beautiful." I leaned over the bar to kiss her softly. "You doing okay over here?"

She nodded and smiled. "Angelo was just telling me about when you guys were growing up."

I groaned. My brothers and I had gotten up to all kinds of shit with Angelo and his sisters growing up.

Lexie giggled knowingly. "Yup... he was just telling me about what happened with the old lady and her cat from down the street."

I chuckled at the memory. "Hey, that damn cat came down eventually, but old Mrs. Evans held that grudge forever."

Angelo nodded in agreement, his eyes crinkled with laughter.

"Could you do me a solid, man, watch the bar for ten?" I asked him with a flick of my head.

"Yeah, sure." He waved his hand dismissively like it was no big deal. "Where are you going?"

I turned to Lex. "I was hoping I could convince this one to join me on the dance floor."

Her eyes widened in surprise. "Oh, hell yes."

Angelo laughed at her response.

I rounded the end of the bar and held out my hand to help Lexie down from her stool. 'Swalla' by Jason Derulo began pumping from the sound system as I towed her out to the center of the crowded dance floor.

Perfect.

This song had an insane beat.

I stopped and held Lexie by the hand, so her arm was stretched up high.

She strutted right around me in a circle, all sass and sex appeal. She spun around when she reached my front and pressed her back up against me.

My arms wrapped around her instinctively and we moved to the beat in unison, her ass grinding against my crotch.

I groaned in her ear. "Damn, baby."

I felt the vibration of her laughing against my chest.

She tilted her head back and looked up at me with her beautiful face.

I leaned in to kiss her, and it was as though the whole world fell away. I felt like I was watching us from above, the crush of bodies around us nothing but a blur around a spotlight, and in the center it was just me and her.

I'd never experienced anything like this before.

Lexie turned in my arms, so her front was pressed against mine, our lips never breaking contact as her delicate hands clasped around my neck.

The song, the dance, my job... it was all forgotten as I slipped my tongue into her mouth and met hers.

I couldn't get enough. My hands found her hips and gripped tight, lifting her slightly off the ground. She was as close to me as she could possibly be, but it still wasn't enough.

She sighed into my mouth, and I knew she could feel it too.

I set her back down and our lips broke apart but stayed close, our heavy breaths mingling together between us.

"I thought you brought me out here to dance," she murmured as the song ended and the A-Trak remix of Lorde's 'Magnets' began.

Our bodies might have been still, but our souls... those were dancing.

"You want to dance, babe?" I asked her.

She nodded, her eyes trained on mine.

If my girl wanted to dance, we'd dance.

I grabbed her, ballroom style and turned her around and around, the crowd taking notice and making space for us.

I ignored the beat as I swept and turned a giggling Lexie around the floor.

The song ended and I dipped her low, kissing her hard as I did. I could feel her smile against my lips and I knew nothing else in my life could compare to the feeling of making this woman happy.

The people that had surrounded us clapped and cheered as I took a bow.

Lexie blushed bright red and tucked her face into my chest with an embarrassed little giggle.

Jason Derulo's 'X2CU' came on and I was making a mental note to talk to the DJ about overdoing the Derulo, when Lexie started laughing uncontrollably.

"What's so funny?" I asked her loudly, trying to be heard over the music.

She pushed up on her toes and tried to explain in my ear, but it was too noisy out here for me to hear what she was saying.

I held one finger up, indicating that she should hang on, and led her out of the madness and back towards the bar where we would have a much better shot at having a conversation.

She was still grinning like a loon when we got there, and I could tell she was on the verge of bursting into laughter again.

I turned her and backed her up so she was pressed against the wall, me towering over her, my arms caging her in.

She gasped, and the cheeky grin on her face fell away. I watched as her eyes roamed over the tense muscles of my arms, her teeth sinking into her bottom lip as she did.

Damn, baby.

The look in her eyes made me momentarily forget what we'd come over here for.

I stared at her, just taking my fill, until something caught her attention and a slow grin spread across her face.

"Didn't you have a question?" she asked with a sly smirk and a giggle.

I smirked back. "You gonna tell me what's so damn funny, or am I gonna have to drag it out of you?"

She pretended to ponder my offer for a moment.

"It's the song." She laughed. "When we first met, I thought it sounded like it should have been the soundtrack for you and your attempts to get me into bed for revenge," she explained.

I listened to the lyrics for a moment.

I just want my ex to see you...

She's not wrong.

I thought back to the first time I met Lexie and smiled. It was hard to think that I'd still been a little hung-up on Quinn. I chuckled as I recalled propositioning Lexie and her calling me out on my bullshit. It was even harder to fathom that it was only a few short days ago.

It seems like a lifetime...

I was so utterly absorbed with Lexie that no other woman even crossed my mind anymore.

I chuckled. "Can't argue with you about that one."

"What's the theme song of your life now?" she asked, her voice a mixture of curiosity and nerves.

Every single love song I knew flashed through my mind, but I reigned it in and went for a light option.

I grinned, deliberately looking her up and down. "Ed Sheeran – Shape of you." I told her as I gestured to the fine body she was teasing me with.

She swatted my shoulder playfully. "Good choice, Mr. Hunt... good choice."

I swooped in and claimed her lips, much to the delight of my staff, who apparently were watching exactly what we were doing, if the whoops and hollers that were being fired in our direction were anything to go by.

"Boss man, you sly dog," I heard Michelle call out.

I chuckled and pulled back from Lexie. "I better go reign in the troops," I told her, already reluctant to have her out of my arms.

She giggled and peeked over her shoulder at my staff. "Go on, boss man," she teased.

I placed another chaste kiss to her lips and stepped away.

"Alright, boys and girls, show's over," I called over my shoulder with a smirk. "Get back to work."

***

"That girl is an absolute hoot." Angelo chuckled. He had come behind the bar to give me his approval of Lexie while she was in the bathroom.

"A little kooky..." he added. "But I like her."

"She's pretty great, right?" I smiled, just the mention of Lexie's name enough to make me break out in a grin.

He studied my face for a moment and then pulled me in for a hug. He patted me on the back before letting me go again.

"What was that for?"

"It's just nice seeing you in a good place, man," he replied genuinely.

It's nice being in a good place.

I tried to wave away his comment like it was no big deal, but he just narrowed his eyes at me. "I'm serious, you know. That shit with your brother and Quinn... hell, I'm still disappointed in him for that, but seeing you happy might just get me over it."

"You should let it go," I encouraged. "Harrison never wanted to hurt me, neither did Quinn... it's just the way things work out sometimes... I'm over it, truly," I told him.

And I was – I was one hundred percent over the fact that Quinn and Harrison were together.

"I can see that." He clapped me on the shoulder as he turned to leave. "A blind man could see how good the two of you are together, man, so congratulations."

***

"You really like working with people, huh?" Lexie asked from where she sat on the bar, her legs dangling.

We'd been closed for nearly an hour and I was nearly ready to get the hell out of here with my girl. That round on the dance floor earlier had me on edge to get her home and into bed so our night could really start.

I grinned at her question and nodded. "Yeah, there's something exciting about working in a club, everyone is so pumped, ya know? It just puts me in a good mood."

"I like it too."

"The club scene?" I asked her as I loaded the last of the empty glasses onto a tray.

"Nah." She shook her head. "I mean it's okay, but mainly I just like watching you; you're so excited, it's really cute." She scrunched up her nose in that way girls did when they looked at a cute little puppy or kitten – in this case, I was the puppy.

I chuckled. "It's a pain in the ass really, getting all jacked up like this…it always keeps me awake for ages after a shift."

"I can think of plenty of things we can do if you can't sleep…" Lexie not-so-subtly hinted.

Me too, baby, me too.

"I like where your head's at," I replied, my tone gruff.

We need to get out of here.

I sat the tray of glasses down – some other sucker could take care of those – and stalked over to where Lexie was perched. I fitted my hips snugly in between her sexy legs and wrapped her in my arms.

She giggled softly and rested her arms around my neck like she always did.

"Thank you for coming here with me," I murmured into her neck. It was strange being on level heights, I'd grown so accustomed to bending down to reach her.

"Thank you for bringing me," she replied softly against my ear. "I had fun."

I knew she wasn't just saying that. Lexie wasn't one of those high maintenance girls who needed tending to every few seconds, just to be kept happy. I could see that she was genuinely content just to be here with me, and I loved her for that.

I was struck once again at just how right it felt, being with her.

Life together would be amazing.

Easy…

Perfect...

Now I just had to figure out a way to make it happen.

***

"Mmmm, Colton..." Lexie moaned my name beneath me.

I chuckled against the soft skin of her belly. "Yeah, baby?"

"More," she demanded – her breathing becoming more labored by the second. "Just... *more*," she begged.

I loved it when she pleaded with me. I loved it even more when she got all incoherent-sounding like she was right now.

"More what?"

"Colt..." she moaned as I kissed her now-pebbled skin. "Please," she begged again.

I've got you, girl.

I pumped into her again with my fingers and she writhed beneath me.

"Oh... god," she mumbled.

I was so hard. Watching her naked body... hearing her sweet sighs... just having her here with me and willing was almost too much to deal with.

"Are you ready for me, baby?"

"I was ready before you even touched me," she moaned.

She wasn't joking; we'd barely made it into my office. We never stood a chance of making it all the way back to my place. I was as close to losing it as she was, some kind of carnal impulse was spurring me on right now and I needed to take her.

Right now.

I slipped my fingers out of her and she groaned at the loss of contact.

"Shhh, baby," I soothed her. "I'll be back."

I found my jeans halfway across the room, thrown haphazardly on top of my filing cabinet. Our clothes had been disregarded in a hasty, lust-filled haze.

I grabbed the condom from my wallet and ripped the foil packet open.

Lexie watched my every move as I prowled back towards her, rolling the rubber down my hard length.

She was draped across the couch in my office, one hundred percent naked.

Absolute perfection.

I was aching for her. I was a man who had always thoroughly enjoyed sex, but I'd never needed a woman the way I did Lexie. She brought out desires in me that I didn't know I possessed.

"Has everyone gone home?" Lexie whimpered as I grabbed her ankles and lifted them up towards my shoulders.

"Nope," I ground out as I lined up and pushed inside her in one fluid stroke. *And I don't give a fuck.*

"Mmmmm," she moaned as I filled her.

I pushed in to the hilt, dragged myself slowly back out and thrust into her again.

"Fuck, babe." My voice was so loud and gruff I barely recognized it as my own.

"Sshhhh," she replied, with a moan. "They'll hear us."

I looked her dead in the eye as I thrust into her again. "Let them hear," I taunted.

Her eyes widened slowly, and I watched as she let go of her inhibitions and relaxed.

I gave exactly zero fucks if my employees heard me in here with Lexie. She was mine, and if I wanted to bang her in my office, I would.

"Let the whole damn world hear," I ground out. "Let them all hear that you're mine."

"Yes!" Lexie cried out.

"Let me hear you, baby," I demanded as I thrust into her over and over.

"Yes!" she cried out again, now writhing beneath me. "Oh, Colt, yes!"

I was so close to the edge, I was barely hanging on.

"I'm gonna lose it, Lex." The words fell from my mouth in the same moment that she cried out with her release.

Just knowing she'd gone over the edge was all it took for me to follow her.

I came hard, so hard I swear I saw stars.

I let her legs slide down and relax as I slumped forward on top of her, breathing hard.

I swept a stray strand of hair from her face and kissed the tip of her nose.

"Let's get out of here quick." She grinned once she'd caught her breath. "I think the whole building would have heard that."

Completely worth it.

***

"What do you want to do today?" I asked her gently as I brushed her messy, sleep-mused hair off her face.

Our last full day together.

We were still in bed, and truth be told, I would have been a happy man if we didn't have to move an inch today, but I knew that was just me being selfish. Lexie needed to see her friends at some point, and I needed to let them know that I'd be taking her to the airport, alone.

That wasn't me being selfish, it was me being smart. I knew Lexie was going to lose it when the time came, and if Ellerslie, Quinn and I were all there, I was worried she wouldn't go.

The idea of her staying was perfect in theory, but I couldn't do it to her. She'd worked so hard to get where she was in her job, and I couldn't, I *wouldn't* ask her to give that up.

We would make this work somehow, but not at the expense of Lexie's career.

"Whatever you want to do..." she answered in a voice that was barely above a whisper.

"Babe, you decide, it's your las—"

"Don't say it," she interrupted me, her voice breaking. "*Please* don't say it."

I could literally feel my heart splitting in two. I was such a fool for thinking I'd truly been in love before now.

Compared to this, I'd barely even known what love was. I knew that now.

This was love. And here I was, too chicken-shit to say the words to the only woman I'd ever really felt it with. It was ironic really, I'd spurted those words off with no real knowledge of their true meaning, and now that I finally understood what they meant, the hypothetical cat had my tongue.

"It'll be okay, babe," I promised her, kissing the side of her head that wasn't pressed against my chest. "Let me treat you to a day you'll never forget."

She turned so she was looking right into my eyes and a lump formed in my throat.

She's just so damn beautiful.

"I will never forget a single moment I spend with you," she told me, a fierce note to her voice that I wasn't accustomed to hearing.

I was certain I wouldn't either. I just wished we didn't have to give each other the chance to test the theory.

"Then let's go do something worth remembering."

23. Lexie

I snapped another picture of the stunning lake with my camera and tucked the undeveloped Polaroid into my pocket.

I wanted to make sure I would remember every single little thing about my time here with Colt.

"Are you hungry, babe?" Colt called to me from the picnic blanket he'd set up on a semi-private spot of the public garden. We'd spent the morning wandering around the common and the gardens, hand-in-hand, just talking and enjoying each other's company.

It was such a pretty spot here and I couldn't have picked a better way to spend my last day. This place felt like the living, breathing, heart of the city.

I looked over at him and my pulse sped up instantly, seeing him reclined on that same blanket, was like a direct flashback to our first date.

I smiled as I thought about it. I still couldn't believe I'd nearly given up on this.

On us.

If it hadn't been for Quinn, I may never have had the balls to go after what I wanted.

Colt.

He was what I wanted. He was the man I could imagine a future with, he was the man I could envision having a life with... having children with. He was who I wanted to wake up next to everyday.

I felt tears welling in my eyes as the reality of our situation hit me yet again. I blinked them back as quickly as I could, not wanting Colt to see me upset over this anymore than he already had.

I was his and he was mine – we'd make this work... somehow. Even if it meant living in separate cities for a year, we'd make it work.

My stomach lurched at the thought of having him so far away, but I knew I would do what I had to do to keep him. Having Colt in my life, in any way, shape or form, was better than not having him at all.

"Lex?" Colt called again, and I realized I'd been frozen to the spot, just staring at him.

I blinked back my tears once more and smiled.

Enjoy the here and now.

Colt smiled back at me, his blond hair all mussed and sexy, and his golden eyes alight with joy.

"Coming," I called back.

I glanced around behind me once more and felt an overwhelming sense of gratitude for where I was right now.

Here with him.

There was nowhere in the world I'd rather be.

*****

"What time are you coming over?" Quinn said by way of hello.

"Coming over for what?" I asked her down the phone.

I looked at Colt for a hint, but he just shrugged.

"If you thought you were getting out of here without one last dinner, then you're as nuts as that old geezer that used to come to that tap class we took."

I giggled at the memory. That old guy really was bat-shit crazy.

I rolled my eyes and smiled. "When and where?"

I heard Quinn clapping gleefully. "El and Law's, any time after five."

"We'll be there," I promised.

"Perfect."

"C'ya then, Q."

I was just about to hang up when I heard Quinn speak again.

"Lex?" Her voice was wary.

"Yeah?"

"It's... I just wanted to tell you that it's good to see you so happy. You and Colton are really good for each other."

I suddenly felt teary-eyed again. It wasn't exactly like Quinn to get too sentimental, especially on her own accord, so I valued her words.

"Thank you," I whispered.

Quinn cleared her throat, and I had a feeling she might have been feeling a little teary too. "See you tonight, girl."

I hung up the phone and clutched it to my chest. I really missed Quinn and El. They were by no means my longest friendships, but they had quickly become some of my closest. The two of them moving out here had left a big hole in my life – a hole that had been filled this past week.

I glanced at Colt, who was looking at me in question.

"Oh shit, I'm so sorry, I just totally said you'd be there without even asking you first," I admitted sheepishly.

He chuckled. "Are you going to be there?"

I nodded. "Of course."

"Then so am I," he replied simply, placing a kiss on the top of my head.

Oh god... sweet much?

"But just so I know, where exactly are we going?"

"Dinner at El's." I beamed. "I'm so excited to see Stella again."

"She's a cute kid."

"The cutest," I agreed as I swung our hands between us.

He smiled down at me, the sun pooling around his face, and I felt the last part of my heart fall in love with Colton Hunt.

"Time and good friends are two things that become more valuable the older
you get."
- Author unknown

24. Colt

We strolled up the path to El and Lawson's front door hand-in-hand. The door swung open, revealing Stella and the dogs waiting to greet us. The dogs actually looked more like they were willing to sacrifice their lives to protect Stella from any unwelcome intruders.

It was pretty sweet really, Stella was trying to push past the big dogs and come outside, but they took turns nudging her back inside with their heads.

"Frank, Zeph – relax," Lawson's voice commanded from inside the house, and the dogs instantly backed off.

"Wawax," Stella mimicked, patting each dog on their head.

"Stella!" Lexie yelled out to her, her excitement obvious.

"Wex, here!" Stella cried, running in her cute toddler way down to see us.

Lexie held out her arms and Stella ran straight into her, hugging her tight.

"Baby girl, those are some big bad guard dogs you've got there." Lexie tickled Stella's ribs as she carried her towards the door.

Stella giggled and squirmed.

"Hey, Stella." I smiled at the angelic little blonde girl. "You might not remember me, I'm Colt."

"Cwolt," she repeated back to me with a toothy grin.

Oh yeah, Lexie was right, this little girl was the cutest.

"Dadda!" she cried excitedly. "Wex and Cwolt here!"

Lawson chuckled. "I can see that, princess."

"How's it going, man?" I shook Lawson's hand when we reached the door of their beautiful home.

"Couldn't be better," he replied as he took Stella, who was stretching out for him, from Lexie.

He kissed her cheek. The love he had for that little girl was obvious for the whole world to see. Stella might not have been his biological daughter, but he was one hundred percent her daddy.

I want that.

The realization of just how much I wanted that hit me like a punch in the nose. It wasn't that I wanted it now, not right this minute – but one day soon, I wanted to feel that same kind of love for my child.

"Stella, you wanna go tell your momma that they're here?" Lawson asked her.

Stella nodded enthusiastically.

He set her down and she took off, presumably to find El.

"She's so beautiful, Lawson," Lexie gushed.

Lawson smiled after his daughter. "Yeah, she sure is," he agreed. "God, it goes so damn quickly, it's hard to believe she's already walking and talking. I swear, you blink and you'll miss it." He sighed.

I squeezed Lexie's hand, feeling surprisingly moved by the emotion in Lawson's voice.

"Anyway, enough gushing over my little princess, come on in."

***

I looked around the full dining table and smiled.

This is how it should be.

This was one of those things that should have been a once a week gathering. I could picture Lexie and I hosting these dinners for everyone in our own home. I could picture us living in something small but cozy, with our own yard and space for a garden out the back... maybe somewhere on the outskirts of town.

I knew I was getting ahead of myself, but right now I didn't care. I was going to let myself have this moment of fantasizing about what life with Lexie could be like.

What it should be like.

Stella, grabbing a handful of mashed potato and shoving it into her mouth, pulled me from my thoughts.

"Ugh, Stella!" El laughed. "Use a fork, honey."

Stella picked up her fork, grabbed another handful of potato and tried to squish it onto the fork.

Everyone cracked up laughing.

"That's not exactly what I had in mind." El giggled, getting up to help her daughter.

"Am I a terrible person for finding that adorable and for hoping she'll do it again?" Lexie whispered to me.

I chuckled. "Well if it does, then we're both bad people."

"It's always funny when it's not your kid," Ellerslie told us. "You just wait until you've got your own one day."

Bring it on.

I peeked at Lexie, she was still watching Stella's every move with amusement.

"That's the Pierce coming out in her," Quinn announced proudly. "Right, Stella girl? Loving those carbs."

"Warbs," Stella repeated.

Harrison laughed. "Just like her aunty."

I had to agree, for such a skinny little thing; Quinn sure put away a ton of food.

Ellerslie turned to grab the wipes off the side table at the same time that Stella decided to grab another handful of her dinner. This time she was inspired to smear it all through her hair.

"Princess!" Lawson groaned.

The rest of us exploded into laughter.

El turned around – wipes in hand. "Oh, Stella! Are you serious?"

Stella grinned at her and El bit back a smile.

She dropped the wipes to the table with a thud. "You may as well finish it off, baby girl, then Daddy can take you out back and hose you down afterwards," she joked.

Stella clapped her hands together gleefully and sent mashed potato flying all over the show.

"It's in my hair," Quinn moaned as she tried to fish the lumps of food off her head.

Lexie giggled and tried to hide it by burying her face in my shoulder.

One look at Harrison attempting to scoop mash out of Quinn's hair with a spoon – a giant grin on his face, was all it took to push me over the edge.

"We're definitely terrible people." I chuckled, as I tucked my face into her hair. "We're going straight to hell."

Lexie looked up at me and smiled a beautiful smile. "Well if you're going to be there, then so am I."

****

Lexie had just excused herself to go to the bathroom and I decided that this was probably the best opportunity I was going to get to talk to Quinn and Ellerslie about the airport tomorrow.

"Can I talk to you both in private for a minute?" I asked the girls as soon as I knew Lex would have been out of earshot.

I gestured towards the living room and they both followed me through.

"I just wanted to talk to you both about Lexie leaving tomorrow."

"Flight's at midday, right?" Quinn replied.

"If you could get her there, we can just meet you? We'll go straight from the office," El added.

I took a deep breath. The two women standing in front of me were by all accounts strong and independent – they weren't the type of women that were used to being told what to do. I knew I was going to need to tread carefully if I wanted to get out of this alive.

"That's actually what I wanted to talk to you both about. I think it might be best for Lexie if you all said your goodbyes tonight. Less stress for her tomorrow, ya know?"

Quinn's eyes narrowed at me instantly, and I knew she already had her back up.

"You're trying to tell us we're not welcome at the airport," she hissed the accusation at me.

Fuck my life.

I looked at El in an attempt to get some support, but she didn't look much happier with me than Quinn did.

Screw it.

If I was going to get my way, I was going to have to find my balls and stand up for what I knew was the right thing for my girl.

"It's not about being welcome, Quinn." I sighed. "It's about what is best for Lexie."

"How can her two best friends not being there, be what's best for her?" Quinn cried.

"Because she's not coping," I snapped back at her.

Deep breath.

"You should have seen her in the park today," I explained gently, more in control of myself now. "She's tearing up all the time... she's really worried that the distance will come between us."

I risked glancing between the two of them. El was now watching me carefully; a look of sympathy in her eyes. Quinn still looked pissed as hell.

"I know how hard it's going to be tomorrow, for her and for me... and I'm pretty sure that if she turns back and sees the three of us standing there, then she won't get on that plane."

"And that would be a bad thing, why?" Quinn demanded.

I shook my head. "I couldn't live with myself if she gave up her job and her life without really thinking it through. It's not that I wouldn't want her here," I assured them. "I want that more than *anything*. But her and I... we can make this work until we figure something out; she's my girl now, and I need you to trust that I'm doing what's best for her."

It won't be easy, but we can do it.

I heard a rustling noise in the hall behind me, but when I turned and looked, there was no one there.

Quinn opened her mouth to argue, but I cut her off.

"I don't want Lexie to have any regrets, and I know that she would regret just dropping her life and walking out on her job with no notice. That's not the kind of person she is."

I could feel myself getting emotional now. I knew she had to get on that flight, but that didn't make it any easier to stomach.

"You're right," El replied quietly, surprising me.

"But—" Quinn tried to argue.

"He's right." El looked her in the eye. "He's doing what's best for Lex, and in this case, it's having us say our goodbyes tonight."

They stared off for a few beats before Quinn caved.

"Okay... fine," she grumbled. "But I can tell you one thing." She spoke quietly. "In a few days you're going to wish we'd gone to that airport and convinced her to stay."

I swallowed the lump in my throat, already knowing that she was dead right, but torn between wanting Lexie to stay, and doing what I knew was the right thing.

"I know what a man looks like when he loves a woman, Colt, and I don't know how you think you're going to live without her, but I hope you find a way to make it work, I truly do," she added before giving me a small smile and turning to walk away.

El squeezed my arm in sympathy and followed Q back into the kitchen.

Tears stung the corners of my eyes and I tried my hardest to blink them back.

Get it together.

I couldn't upset Lexie now, no matter how badly I was hurting.

"I think you've really got to wait and see how things play out. Sometimes a decision you might consider a regret or failure in the present can turn out to be the catalyst for something extraordinary in the end.
Some of life's wildest journeys begin with a wrong turn."
- Beau Taplin

25. Lexie

"Do you believe in fate?" I asked him as I snuggled in even closer to his warm, hard body.

He lay still for a moment, the only movement the rise and fall of his chest beneath my cheek.

"Yeah, I think I do," he finally answered.

"Yeah?" I replied, tracing light patterns on his bare abdomen.

"Yeah... you gotta believe in something, right?"

"I guess so," I agreed.

"Well, *something* brought you to me." His voice turned husky. "And I don't know if it was fate, or divine intervention or whatever else..."

He rolled me onto my back so he was leaning over me, looking right into my eyes.

"But whatever it was, Lex, I owe it for that. I owe it for giving me you."

My heart felt like it was going to explode. I didn't know what good I'd done to deserve this man...

Some seriously good karma had come my way.

I sighed.

And then some bad karma...

I must have done something pretty shitty in a past life to make me deserve the goodbye we would be forced to have when I boarded that plane at midday tomorrow without him.

This wasn't fair. You aren't meant to find the person you want to share your entire life with and then have to walk away from them.

This is what I was afraid of.

"Don't, little bird, don't get yourself upset again," he told me, sensing that I was heading for a meltdown. "We'll make it work somehow; I'm not letting you go," he promised.

He knows me so well already.

I lay back down, content in his arms, just listening to the beating of his heart for a moment to regather myself.

"I don't know if it's just because we're on borrowed time that it all feels so... *intense*..." I ran my fingertips gently over his jaw. "Do you think if we had forever that it would still feel like this?" I asked him timidly.

"All I know," he told me softly as he stared deep into my eyes. "Is that *this* is the most real thing in my life and there's not even one reason I can see, that we can't have forever, okay?"

God I hope he's right.

I nodded. "It's just you and me."

He kissed my lips softly. "It's just you and me," he repeated back to me.

***

"Just get one shift done, baby," Colt encouraged. "That's what? Only a few weeks away? And we'll make plans to see each other as soon as you get back on dry land, okay?"

I nodded.

I couldn't talk.

I'll lose it.

At this point I was already borderline hysterical.

Not Colt, he's staying strong for me.

It was no secret that I wasn't coping. He'd even banned El and Quinn from coming to the airport; I'd overheard him begging and reasoning with them last night.

Until I nearly got caught eavesdropping.

He knew that it was going to be too much for me today, and he was right. I was barely keeping it together as it was, if they were here too, it would have been that much harder to set foot on that plane. We'd said our goodbyes last night, and that had been hard enough.

I'm going to miss them so much.

I didn't feel like I was going home, I felt like I was *leaving* my home. It wasn't so much about the place as it was about the people – or more specifically one person in particular. Colt was my home now.

I sobbed quietly, trying my best to be strong and failing miserably.

"*Please* don't cry," Colt begged me, his face a tortured mask. "I'm trying to be strong for you, Lex, but I can't handle your tears, baby, they'll break me."

"I'm... sorry," I told him between sobs as I desperately tried to reign it in.

He pulled into the parking lot of the airport and slowly switched off the engine. He turned in his seat to look at me.

"Lexie, baby, are you going to be okay?"

I forced myself to be brave and look into his eyes. His beautiful golden eyes were rimmed with unshed tears and it broke my heart. But even now, his only concern was me and my emotions – he really was the most amazing man I'd ever met.

"I miss you already," I told him, my voice cracking with emotion.

"I miss you too," he replied quietly.

We sat there, just staring at one another for what felt like forever. I didn't know what was going through his head, but me... I was memorizing every single detail about him.

The way his silky hair sat... the shape of his jaw... the curve of his nose... his perfect, soft lips... the way his hazel eyes were flecked with gold.

"Why does this feel like goodbye?" I whispered.

"Oh, baby, it's not really goodbye... not forever."

Another sob escaped my control.

"Come here," he instructed, patting his lap.

I threw off my seatbelt and scrambled over the center console and into his lap.

His arms came around me like a vise, holding me tight. I'd never felt safer than I did in that moment, which was crazy – considering I was about to leave him.

"I promise you, Lexie Chase, I'll see you as soon as we can make it work." His words were muffled as he spoke against my shoulder. "This is *not* goodbye; it's just... see you soon."

I let out a snuffled laugh. "You sound like some kind of cliché quote."

"I don't care – it made you smile," he boasted.

"You always make me smile."

We sat, me in his lap, just holding one another for a few minutes, Colt rubbing slow, relaxing circles on my back.

"This isn't the end, baby; you and me are just getting started."

"I know," I agreed with a sniff. And I did know that. But it didn't make this any easier.

We fell into silence again.

"I'd better go," I finally said with a sigh. "I'll miss my flight."

Colt let out a devastated groan.

I sat back so I could look at him again.

I love you.

I wanted to tell him, but I couldn't, the words got caught in my throat and wouldn't come out. I was scared – scared it would make this too hard, and scared he wouldn't be able to say it back to me.

His hands went straight to my face, clasping it gently in his safe hands. "You mean *everything* to me."

"I know." I sniffed.

Our mouths met in a kiss filled with love, lust, pain and promise. It was like nothing I'd ever experienced. I kissed him like it just might be the last time and he gave as good as he got in return.

We were both breathless by the time our lips had finished telling each other goodbye.

"I'll get your bag," Colt whispered sadly.

***

Colt jogged back over from where he'd been chatting with one of the airline staff, I had no idea what it was about, but that was Colt for you... the man was full of surprises, and I didn't doubt that his conversation had been anything other than the organization of a surprise for me. I hadn't seen him get his wallet out, so at least I knew he wasn't wasting his money on me.

He slowed his jog to more of a prowl and I felt my belly clench.

The things that man does to me...

I hadn't expected him to come in here with me. I'd thought we were saying goodbye in the car and that I was going to be left to fall apart without an audience.

Colt had informed me, however, that if I was going to kiss him like that, then he was coming back for seconds.

So here we are.

"What was that about?" I quizzed him as he reached me and fitted me back into his arms.

He tapped the end of my nose and grinned. "Never you mind, little bird, never you mind."

"What did you do?" I scolded in mock outrage.

"What makes you think I did anything?" he asked, his face the picture of innocence.

"Because I know you better than you think." I giggled.

He squeezed me tight and replied, his voice hoarse in my ear. "You have no idea how lucky I am to have you, Lex."

He was dead wrong about that. I was the lucky one to know him, and have him know me. This week had been, without a doubt, the best of my life.

"I guess this is it." I shrugged.

I had my ticket in my hand, and Colt couldn't come with me through the security check. This was the moment I had to leave the man I was totally and utterly in love with, and go back to my life like it had never happened.

No.

Nothing will be like it was before.

"I made you something," he told me shyly, digging his hand into his pocket.

"What is it?" I asked in a whisper. I had a feeling that whatever this was just might have had the power to push me over the edge.

"You'll have to wait until you get home." He pressed a USB stick into my waiting hand.

I sighed in relief.

He really had thought of everything. I had no doubt that he was well aware of the fact I wouldn't be able to deal with anything sentimental right now, so he'd given me something I couldn't access until I was alone and in the comfort of my own apartment.

"Thank you." I pushed up to my toes and kissed his soft lips.

"*Anything* for you, Lexie," he told me genuinely.

"I'll see you soon?" I asked timidly.

"You can count on it," he promised as he kissed me again, and I knew this time, it was the last one.

I looked into his eyes one last time before turning and walking away.

I didn't look back, I couldn't. Tears were streaming down my face faster than I could swipe them away, and I knew if I turned back, I'd go back, and there would be no getting on that plane.

My heart was screaming at me to turn around, but my head assured me that this was the way it was meant to be.

Why does it hurt so damn much?

I knew the answer to that question, if I was really being honest with myself.

I love him.

I loved him more than anything else in my life. More than my job, more than my life back home, more than *anything*... it had taken me less than one week to fall head over heels in love with Colton Hunt, and I knew without a doubt that it was the kind of love a person never really got over.

"I love you," I whispered to the floor.

***

The USB port on the panel in front of me was taunting me. I knew it was a bad idea to put that stick in there right now, surrounded by a plane full of strangers, but I couldn't seem to get the message to my hands, as they uncapped it and plugged it into the port.

I slipped my earphones into my ears and waited as it loaded up, my knee jiggling nervously up and down.

This was a bad idea. I'd only just managed to stop the fresh wave of tears that had started when I'd discovered that Colt had sweet-talked someone at the ticket counter into bumping me up to first class.

That was the only reason I was even considering looking at whatever Colt had given me now, rather than waiting until I got home. First class was a hell of a lot more private than coach, and my little booth was providing me with a sense of security – even if it was a false one.

The screen flickered to life and revealed that there was only one file on the stick – a video file.

I tapped on it nervously, snuggling further down into the blanket I'd been given.

The file opened and I could just make out Colt's face, looking at the screen in a dark room. He held his finger up to his lips, indicating for me to be quiet. He held the phone out, revealing a sleeping me in the bed he'd just got out of.

I giggled.

What is he doing?

He crept out of the room and shut the door behind himself. "Hey, baby," he whispered to the camera.

I reached out and stroked a finger down the side of his face.

"I've got a surprise for you, and I didn't want sleeping you to find out." He chuckled. "I'm confusing myself, present you, future you, whatever, this is for you, my little song bird."

He sat the phone down on the coffee table in his living room, before sitting on the couch and adjusting the phone to ensure he could be seen on the screen.

He slipped his glasses on and my heart fluttered.

He grabbed his guitar from next to the couch and slung it into his arms, before starting to strum it gently.

I recognized it instantly as 'Tenerife Sea'.

He sang every word so beautifully, looking right into the camera with a sweet smile, the one that seemed to be reserved only for me.

I was shocked... *mind blown...* totally and utterly stunned. I couldn't believe I'd slept through this, I couldn't believe he'd done this for me.

My heart skipped a beat.

Does he? Is he telling me he loves me?

I had a pretty good feeling that he felt the exact same way I did. I loved him completely. But I also knew that it would have made the situation so much harder for the both of us if we had said those words aloud.

He finished the song and I could tell he was battling with his emotions the same way I was right now. He'd poured everything into that song, I loved Ed Sheeran, but my boyfriend had just given him a run for his money.

He placed the guitar back down next to the couch and picked up his phone. He crept back down the hallway, opened the door to his bedroom quietly and snuck back into bed. He leaned over and placed a kiss on my sleeping head and blew a kiss to his phone.

Then the screen went black.

I squeezed my eyes tight and cried for what felt like forever.

"And before he walked away he whispered to me "Just because the timing is off does not mean that you and I are not destined to be. There is no end to our story.""

- Natalie Jensen

26. Colt

My life right now was like the scene in the movie where they played the montage of the guy after he's lost the love of his life. The one where he's walking around the streets aimlessly, heartbroken and alone. The music is slow and depressing and the weather is cloudy and raining.

Welcome to my life.

Every single damn minute since she'd left had sucked.

There hadn't been even a fraction of a second in which I hadn't thought about her, or missed her, or wanted her to come back.

I didn't even tell her I loved her.

She wasn't coming back though. And I couldn't go to her. I'd never hated the club and the responsibility I had there more than I did right now.

Truthfully, it wasn't the club I hated... I *loved* my job, I loved being around people, especially when they were having a good time... but I hated the ropes that were currently tying me down to the job.

If it weren't for this job – mine and my brother's investment, I'd be there by now.

I'd be with her.

My phone rang and I hoped, like always, that it was Lexie. I knew it wouldn't be though, I was up early, and she was three hours behind. My girl liked her sleep too much to be up that early. I put the Polaroid photos of Lexie and me down with a sigh and grabbed my phone.

It was an unknown number, which always made me nervous.

"Hello?" I answered cautiously.

"What kind of welcome is that for your big brother?" the voice demanded.

"Mitch?" I asked in disbelief. I hadn't heard from my brother in what felt like forever. He was in the army and he didn't get in contact often.

"The one and only," he drawled. "Wanna get a coffee?"

Smartass.

"I wasn't planning on flying out to the base today," I drawled.

He was silent for a beat.

"Well it's your lucky day, kiddo."

I heard a knock at my door.

No way.

I jogged down the hall to the door and flung it open, my phone still glued to my ear.

I couldn't believe it. Standing right in front of me, in the flesh, was Mitch.

I hadn't seen him in person for over a year and it hit me like a ton of bricks just how much I'd missed him.

"Holy shit."

"It's good to see you too, bro." He pulled me into a man hug.

"You don't know just how good," I replied.

***

"You gonna spill about this girl or am I gonna have to kick your ass like old times to get it out of you?" He mock punched my arm.

I hadn't realized I was so transparent.

"How'd you know there was a girl?"

"A guy's face looks like that? It's *always* about a girl."

I huffed out a laugh.

We'd been sitting around for about quarter of an hour now, he'd been filling me in on his latest antics at the base and I'd told him about the club. All safe, light subjects.

I flipped him off, but sighed in defeat. "Her name's Lexie."

"Hot name," he replied quickly.

"Give it a rest, man."

"Sorry, carry on." He smirked.

Mitch had always had too much energy. He was older than me by five years, but sometimes I swore he was the least mature of the three of us.

"She's something else, man, sings like an angel, she's beautiful, funny, sexy, kind... and I know you've heard shit like this from me before, but this is different," I insisted. "After Quinn, Harrison told me that one day I'd meet *the one* and that I'd just know. Well, I know. She's it."

"She's the one?"

I nodded. "All it took was seven days."

"Seven days to what?"

I looked him in the eye. "Change my life."

"Shit, man," he acknowledged as he leaned back and spread his arms wide on the back of my couch. "That's some deep shit."

"Yeah." I nodded. "I know."

"So where is she? I wanna meet this sexy Lexie," he replied with a shit-eating grin.

"Jesus." I shook my head. "Don't call her that. And she's not here. She's gone... back home."

"Well that sucks a donkey dick..." he muttered, his voice actually sounding sympathetic for once. "So what are you gonna do about it?"

"You're not going to tell me I'm being stupid?" I asked skeptically. I'd been expecting him to laugh in my face, the same way he had the last time I'd told him I loved a girl. Although, now I could see why he'd laughed at me in the past.

I hadn't been in love at all – not like this.

He shook his head. "Not this time. You look... I dunno... *different*. I guess you look the way I feel when I think about..." he trailed off.

I opened my mouth to ask him what he'd been going to say, but he cut me off.

"So what are you going to do about it, little bro?"

I ran my hand through my hair. "I dunno, man, there's nothing I can do. The club needs me, and I'd never ask her to give up her dream job to be here with me."

"So you'd give up the club if you could?" he asked quizzically.

Hell yes.

"In a heartbeat. I can run a club anywhere," I told him without a moment's hesitation. It was true. The club was nothing to me in comparison to being with Lexie.

His lips spread into a slow, easy grin. "Well then, today really is your lucky day, little bro."

Doesn't feel very lucky.

"And how's that?" I prompted.

"I'm not just here for a visit." He let the words settle for a moment. "I got honorably discharged.... I'm here for good," he explained.

His words hung in the air between us. Mitch had been in the military for as long as I could remember.

"You left the military?" I gaped.

He nodded. "I did."

"Why?" I asked in disbelief. I'd always imagined that he'd be there either until he was old and grey, or until they kicked him out. The 'honorable' part of his discharge assured me that wasn't the case now.

"I met someone too," he answered with a smile, taking me completely by surprise. "Her name's Sophia, we're engaged and she's carrying my son."

Mind explosion.

"I'm sorry, what?" I stared at him blankly, certain I must have misheard him.

He chuckled loudly. "You heard right. I'm all loved up; my woman's got my ring on her finger and my baby in her belly."

"Holy shit."

"Holy shit indeed," he mused.

"I can't form thoughts."

My mind was totally blown. Out of the three of us, I would have thought Mitch was the least likely to be getting married and having kids. But here he was, retired from the army, engaged *and* having a baby.

"I'm moving back," he announced, blowing my mind even further. "Soph is from here too and she wants to be closer to her parents and her sister when the baby comes, which works out well for me."

Finally, some good news after all the shit lately.

"That's awesome. It'll be cool to have you close."

He chuckled again. "But *you* won't be here."

I frowned, not understanding. "Umm... last time I checked, we were sitting in my apartment... I'm pretty sure I live here."

"I'm giving you your out," he stated, his steely gaze focused on mine. "I can take care of the club from here; it'd be about time I pulled my weight there anyway." He pointed at me. "You go get your girl back."

"You want to take over managing the club?" I asked, totally and utterly astonished by the unexpected direction my morning had taken.

"Sure, why not." He shrugged. "Can't be that hard."

I chuckled. He may have been trying to wind me up, but I didn't give a shit. He'd just given me the opportunity I'd been dreaming of ever since I watched my world walk away from me at that airport.

I hadn't been able to bring myself to hire a stranger to run our club, but Mitch... Mitch I knew I could count on.

I stood and he mimicked me. I pulled him in for a hug and clapped him on the back. "Thank you," I told him quietly as we broke apart.

"It's what brothers are for," he insisted.

"How quick do you think you can learn the ropes?" I asked, my mind already whirring with the possibilities.

"I can start as soon as Sophia and I find an apartment."

That might take weeks.

The light bulb flickered to life above my head. "How's this one?" I suggested, gesturing around the space – it wasn't anything fancy, but it was clean and tidy and there would be plenty of space for them for now.

Mitch glanced around and shrugged. "Looks pretty good to me."

"It's all yours," I announced. I wouldn't be needing it anymore anyway.

"Too easy," he drawled. "So now what?"

"I'll give you two days," I offered. "I want to meet this woman of yours, say hey to her and her belly and then get the hell out of here."

"You in some kind of hurry?" He smirked.

"You bet your ass I am," I replied without hesitation.

It's going to be a long two days.

27. Lexie

Everything felt wrong without him in my orbit.

For the first time in my life, I wasn't looking forward to getting on that cruise ship today, I wasn't excited to sing or dance, I wasn't even really looking forward to seeing my friends onboard.

All I wanted to do was sleep, eat, look at our photos and listen to the song he'd sung for me; I knew that I was probably heading to a really unhealthy place if this continued. I knew I needed to get out of my apartment, but I just felt hollow inside.

Colt and I had spoken every day, at least once, and I knew he was doing it as tough as I was. We were both miserable. I'd nearly booked plane tickets back about ten times, but I couldn't seem to hit accept. I had my job here, I'd worked hard to get here, and I knew that I shouldn't just give all that up.

Colt had confessed to nearly up and leaving to come to me too, but his responsibilities to the club made it impossible. He was the one in charge and there was no one to take over for him.

We were both stuck in our own lives.

These had been the longest weeks of my life. I wished that I'd stayed with him until my next shift and spent my free weeks there with him instead of here alone, but at the time I hadn't thought it would be this hard.

I was so wrong.

So here I was, packing for a fifteen-night cruise to the Hawaiian Islands, which I didn't even want to be on anymore.

I probably couldn't recall a single thing that was in that suitcase, I just didn't care. The only items of clothing I cared about anymore were the t-shirts of Colt's I'd snuck into my suitcase before I'd left him.

I abandoned the packing and decided to call Colt. I needed to hear his voice telling me that everything was going to be okay. He was the only thing that could calm me down now.

Tears threatened to well up in my eyes. I'd been so damn emotional these last two weeks, it wasn't like me, but then, I'd never been in love like this before. It had changed me in an irreversible way.

"Hey, this is Colt; leave me a message after the beep."

Dammit. Voicemail.

The shrill beep pierced my ear and I hung up. Colt had been so busy the past few days that we hadn't been able to talk as much as we usually did. He'd blamed it on some changes he had happening at the club... he'd seemed pretty excited about what he had going on. If I was honest, it hurt to think that he was getting on with his life without me.

I called once more, but got the same message.

Back to packing it is...

I trudged into my bathroom and started poking around for my makeup, toothbrush and paste, tampons, hairbrush...

Woah...

Reality hit me like a slap in the face.

Oh shit.

I held the small pink box of tampons in my hands, my heart thumping in my chest.

Oh shit.

I flew back into the bedroom, pulling up the calendar on the screen of my phone.

My period had begun the Saturday before I'd arrived to see Quinn and El. That was about fourteen days before I'd arrived back home. I'd been home for over two and half weeks now.

The numbers swirled in my head.

That was too many days. I had a twenty-eight-day cycle. *Always.*

I was five days late.

Holy shit.

I can't be pregnant...

Can I?

Other than that first time, we'd been careful. And I'd taken a morning-after pill.

They're effective... breathe... it's just a few days.

I wasn't convincing even to myself.

I grabbed my laptop and flipped it open. I hastily typed 'morning-after pill effectiveness' into the search bar and hit enter.

I felt my heart speed up as I read the words on the screen in front of me.

This can't be right...

The first search result stated that if taken within seventy-two hours, the morning-after pill could reduce the risk of pregnancy by up to eighty-nine percent.

Up to eighty-nine percent?

I couldn't breathe. Only *up to* eighty-nine percent...

How was that possible?

I had stupidly believed that I was taking something that was nearly one hundred percent effective.

I scrolled further down the page.

Ninety-five percent effective if taken within twenty-four hours...

Well shit.

After all of our forgetfulness, I certainly hadn't made it within the twenty-four hour cut off.

I clicked on every link the search had found, but the results were still the same.

I am so screwed...

I dialed Colt again, but still got his voicemail.

Oh. My. God.

I needed to take a test. My brain was screaming at me to go and get one, but my body wasn't getting the message.

No, no, no...

Holy shit....

I didn't even need to take a test; I was convinced that I already knew what it would say.

Pregnant.

All the sleeping, eating, the emotions... it all made sense now.

Holy shit.

I needed to talk to Colt.

Take a test first, woman...

The sensible part of my brain took over and I grabbed my keys, some cash and my phone.

I was taking a test, right now.

***

The two bright pink lines stared back at me, taunting me.

I knew it.

Part of me was overjoyed at the fact that I was carrying Colt's baby. He was the only one for me – I had no doubt about that. But the reality of the situation was that we lived thousands of miles apart, and that didn't look set to change anytime in the foreseeable future.

It was already a complicated situation that had just become one thousand times more complicated by this new addition.

I still couldn't get Colt on the phone, and I was beginning to freak out here on my own. I had to be on the ship in forty-five minutes and I still had no idea what I was going to do.

I need Colt.

I needed to let him know what was happening, but I felt overwhelmingly guilty at the prospect of telling him he was going to be a dad over the phone... but I also couldn't get off that godforsaken boat for two whole weeks to be able to do it in person.

What a mess.

I had no idea how he was going to react to this news.

Will he be happy? Angry? Resentful?

What if he thinks I tried to trap him?

My stomach lurched.

What if he doesn't want me anymore?

I stared at the clock on my nightstand and knew I couldn't put off leaving any longer. I couldn't afford to lose my job now.

I threw the rest of my crap into my bag and zipped it up hastily. I took one last look around before I headed downstairs to get on my bike.

Penny will know what to do.

"Everything I've never done, I want to do it with you."
- William Chapman

28. Colt

The six-hour flight had been excruciatingly long. Every hour that passed had me freaking out about not speaking to Lexie, she called me every morning when she woke up and today would have been the first time I hadn't been able to answer.

Lexie had no idea I was coming, so I had no valid reason to explain my disappearance from cell phone service. When I got the chance to call her back, I was probably going to have to blame being busy at work for being the reason I couldn't talk.

I hated lying to her. It went against every instinct I had. I was an honest guy, especially with the people I loved, and Lexie was no exception, but Quinn and El had managed to convince me that I should keep this from her. They'd spouted some rubbish about it being a romantic gesture. Apparently, the element of surprise was key in romantic gestures.

I wasn't so sure, but they'd ganged up on me when I was weak.

Majority rules.

It had only been two days of concealing the truth and I already wasn't coping.

Setting foot outside the terminal in the sweltering heat, I wasn't so sure it was such a great plan after all. I would have killed to have Lexie here waiting for me. I could imagine the way she'd run to me, jump into my arms and kiss me senseless.

But she wasn't here.

I glanced around, not a single clue who or what exactly it was that I was meant to be looking for.

Getting hold of Lexie's friends on the ship had been a bit of a process, but I'd got there in the end. I'd first had to go to Q and El, they'd then contacted Brooke and Stacey, both of whom had been no help, but we struck it lucky with Jemma. Her and her husband Connor had honeymooned on the cruise ship that Lex sang on, and Jemma had made friends with a woman named Penny, who was apparently very close with Lexie.

I'd called Penny myself and she'd been more than excited to help me with pulling off this surprise. She'd even had her own surprise for me, and everything felt like it was finally falling perfectly into place.

I switched my phone on and saw that I had not only one or two, but numerous missed calls from Lexie.

My heart sped up slightly. I was expecting her to have called, just not this many times.

Is something wrong?

There was a text too.

"I tried to call, but I couldn't get you. If you get this message soon, call me back, otherwise I'll call you after the show tonight, okay? I miss you."

I miss you too.

I love you.

I wasn't going to call her back now, the message was from an hour ago and I didn't want to interrupt her if she was getting ready to go to work.

I still didn't know exactly how this was going to play out just yet, but either way I knew I'd be seeing her soon.

A tooting horn pulled me from my thoughts. I looked around to see a beat-up old red hatchback that must have been at least three hundred years old, pulled over, the blinker flashing.

A wild-looking woman with bright blue hair popped up out of the door.

"Colt?" she called out to me.

Penny?

"That's me," I confirmed.

"Well c'mon now, we'll be late." She double tapped the roof of the car before getting back in.

I chuckled to myself, I had not been expecting a sixty-something-year-old woman with hair the color of the sky, but here she was. I grabbed my bag and jogged over to her car. I didn't want to be late. Late for what, I wasn't really sure, but there was only one way to find out.

***

"This is incredible." I glanced around the space before me. I'd never had the opportunity to set foot on a cruise ship before and it was blowing my mind. I hadn't expected it to be so big and spacious.

I could see why Lex was so in love with her life on the sea.

"You like it?" Penny asked.

She'd picked me up and driven us straight over to the port, where we were about to depart – I hadn't realized we were cutting such a fine line, but Penny had promised that the ship wouldn't be going anywhere without her.

I was still pinching myself that this quirky woman was the cruise director. She was in charge of all onboard hospitality, entertainment and social events. She was essentially Lexie's boss, and she was about to become mine too.

"I love it."

"So you'll take the job?" She pressed, her voice full of hope.

"I'll take the job," I confirmed with a smile.

She thought I was helping her out by taking it on such short notice, but really it was the other way around.

"Thank heavens." She pulled me in for a hug. She was so welcoming and warm; it wasn't hard to see why Lexie was so fond of her.

"Do you think she's here yet?" I asked her, not needing to specify who I was referring to.

She glanced at her wrist watch. "She usually gets on at the very last minute, so I'd imagine not quite yet, but she'll be here very soon."

I felt a goofy smile spread across my face. I was dying to see my girl. I couldn't wait to see the look on her face when she realized I'd come here for her.

"But for right now, we've got things to do, lover boy, I need you to meet the bar staff, get you up to speed on protocol..." She looked back and forth between me and the clipboard in her hands. "Oh there's just so much to do. We'll leave the sleeping arrangements until later, if that's okay with you, I'm assuming you'll be sharing my favorite singer's room, but we can't have her spotting your bags now, can we?"

She didn't give me time to get a word in.

"Just put your things in the back room over there." She pointed behind the bar. "We've got a manager's meeting in five, so you can meet the team there, after that we'll get you a uniform and access passes for tomorrow..."

I wasn't sure if she was still talking to me, or if she was making a mental list for herself.

"I'm assuming you want the same schedule as Lexie?" she asked.

"Huh?" I'd let my thoughts wander.

"You only want to work the cruises that Lexie works, right?"

"Oh, yeah, sorry, that would be great, thank you, Penny."

"It's my pleasure." She smiled warmly. "I don't know if you've noticed, but I have quite the soft spot for that girl of yours, and I want nothing more than happiness for her. And if it's not too forward of me to say, you seem like the kind of man who would make her very happy."

I refrained from puffing my chest out like a proud peacock.

"I hope I'll make her happy for a very long time," I told her sincerely."

"Well good." She beamed. "Now let's get going."

I chucked my stuff into the back room as she'd instructed and followed after her.

My phone rang from my pocket as we headed into the manager's meeting and I had no choice but to ignore it.

I grimaced as I thought about Lexie's calls going unanswered, I had a bad feeling in the pit of my stomach that she needed me. She'd told me she would call after her show, and I knew for a fact that she hadn't performed yet.

Maybe it's not even her calling.

"Don't worry, pet, she'll be here soon enough." Penny winked at me, pulling me from my thoughts.

29. Lexie

"Lily, do you know where Penny is?" I popped my head into my neighbor's room. Lily was a jazz pianist in one of the fine-dining restaurants.

"Manager's meeting," she replied as she smacked her freshly painted bright red lips together, staring at her own reflection.

"Still?" I quizzed. The manager's meeting was usually well and truly done by four.

"You didn't hear?" she asked, looking at me through her mirror. "She got a new manager for the Alchemy bar. She'll be showing him the ropes."

Shit.

I only had two hours until I had to sing, and there was no way I'd get hold of her with a new manager to prep.

"Oh... that's good."

"I heard from Kim that he's a *total* babe." She swooned.

"Hmmm," I murmured, not in the least bit interested in the new piece of eye candy the ship had to offer.

"Is everything okay, Lex?" she asked, noticing my less than enthusiastic response.

I shot her a fake smile. "Yeah, everything is great."

***

I smoothed my black dress over my hips. I knew it was all in my head, but it just didn't seem to fit the same anymore. It was like my hips were already widening to make allowances for the baby in my belly.

I'm losing my mind.

I glanced around the restaurant; tonight I was performing a solo cabaret act. Something I did often, but this time I was nervous. I didn't feel like myself anymore. It was as though I'd left a part of myself back on that small V.I.P. in my boyfriends club.

Back with him.

"Two minutes, Lexie girl," Todd, one of the older lighting guys called to me.

I nodded and my stomach churned.

Not now, little baby, not now.

It was only a thirty-minute set.

Thirty minutes and then I can try and call Colt again.

I still hadn't planned out what the hell I would say, but I knew I couldn't keep this from him any longer. I'd known only a few hours, and I was dying to not be alone with this life-changing news anymore.

I need him.

Just how much I needed him hit me so hard in that moment that I had to sit down to stop my head from spinning.

Breathe... just breathe.

"You're up, sweetheart," Todd called to me.

I nodded again and got shakily to my feet.

I can do this.

"True love has a habit of coming back."
- Author unknown

30. Colt

She was near. I could feel it. Excitement coursed through my veins at the prospect of seeing her again, holding her in my arms and breathing in the smell that was one hundred percent Lexie Chase.

I was also nervous. There was this nagging thought in the back of my mind that maybe she wouldn't be happy about me being here. I'd literally shown up in her life, unannounced and uninvited, and if she turned me down... if she wasn't ready for this, it was going to kill me.

I meant what I'd told Mitch – Lexie was the one for me.

I glanced around at the bar – my new job. It was nothing like the club back home, but it was cool. The staff seemed nice and everyone had welcomed me with open arms. Right now, I was just learning the ropes and in the back of my mind, making a list of improvements that would help this place tick over a little better. Penny had informed me that it wasn't performing as well as expected, and because of that, they'd had trouble keeping managers for more than a few months at a time.

Speak of the devil.

Penny smiled brightly at me as she approached the bar. "Take a break," she suggested.

"Me?" I looked around to check she was speaking to me. "I've only been here an hour or two."

She winked at me. "I know, but a certain petite little brunette is on the stage."

My eyes shot up from the bench I was wiping down. "Where?" I demanded softly.

Her tinkling laugh surrounded me. "Just a few doors away, c'mon, I'll show you."

I didn't need telling twice. I dropped the cloth and gave Mikey, the guy helping me get settled, a nod; he gave me a nod and a smirk back – everyone in this place knew about me and Lex already.

Apparently there were no secrets on this cruise ship.

I followed Penny out of the bar and down to a restaurant/lounge area. The sound of Lexie's sweet voice filled my ears and soothed my soul simultaneously. Hearing her voice was like coming home. I paused outside the door and took a deep breath.

Penny nudged my arm and raised her eyebrows at me. "Aren't you coming in? We're just in time for her last song."

Is this how I wanted to surprise her?

I had a feeling that if I walked in there right now, she'd abandon her set to come to me, and that wasn't right. A voice like Lexie's needed to be heard.

I shook my head slowly as I listened to her singing 'All I Want' by Kodaline. Her voice was more haunting than I could remember and she sounded on the verge of breaking down.

Penny must have sensed it too. She gave me a small smile and disappeared around the corner to watch.

I still hadn't laid eyes on her, but I couldn't make myself move. All I could do was listen.

Her voice turned husky and my heart pounded in my chest.

My sweet Lexie.

She was singing from the heart.

A shiver passed over me, leaving a path of goosebumps in its wake.

She sounded so hurt, so alone. Her voice was connecting with every part of me, mirroring the way I felt from being without her.

The crowd inside the room erupted into applause as the song came to an end.

"Thank you," she replied quietly. "I've got time for one last song."

I wasn't sure how much more of this I could take. My heart was breaking for her. Even though I was here now, the guilt at letting her be apart from me was threatening to swallow me whole – she obviously wasn't coping quite the way I thought she was.

The backing track, or maybe it was a live band, I couldn't tell from my hidden spot, started and I recognized the tune as 'What now' by Rihanna. I tried desperately to swallow the lump in my throat – Lexie was hurting, big time.

She sounds like an angel.

Her voice glided effortlessly through the verse.

Nothing, I mean *nothing* would ever compare to hearing the woman I loved, singing like this. This was by no means the first time I'd heard her voice, but in a way it felt like it was, there was so much emotion in her voice, she was feeling the words deep inside her soul – and so was I.

Her voice clogged with tears on the last note and I rounded the corner.

My girl needs me.

I glanced around the room, searching for her, finally spotting her at the far corner of the room; she was being ushered off the stage by Penny, her back to me.

Lexie... my little song bird.

Penny whipped her head around, obviously looking for me. She gestured her head towards the bar and I took it to mean that I should go back to work. She winked and I knew she had a plan.

I just had to hope that she knew what she was doing.

31. Lexie

Thank god for Penny.

She'd bustled me off that stage in her arms before the crowd had realized my tears were more than just for show. She must have seen it in my eyes that I was on the verge of a meltdown, and we both knew that once I started; there would be no stopping me.

"Deep breaths, honey, deep breaths," she coached me. She pressed down on my shoulders until I was seated in a chair in the staff-only area out back.

I sucked in a couple of shallow breaths.

"Can you tell me what's wrong? Or what you need?"

"Colt," I panted out. "I just need to talk to Colt."

"What's happened, sweetie, talk to me," Penny demanded in that soft, soothing way she had.

I took another breath, deeper this time, and tried to focus on Penny, she'd crouched down in front of me so we were at eye level.

I can talk to her, she'll help.

"I'm pregnant," I answered quietly, and for some reason I sounded ashamed. "I couldn't get Colt on the phone... he doesn't know."

Penny's eyes lit up like a proud grandmother. "That's fantastic news." She lightly squeezed my shoulders. "Are you okay? I take it from the look on your face that it wasn't planned?"

I shook my head. "We only had a week together, Pen, what if it was just a holiday fling for him?" I bit down on my lip to try and stop myself from crying.

"Has he done or said anything to make you think that?" she asked, gently coaxing me to see that I was overreacting. Penny was always the voice of reason on this ship.

"No." I shook my head again. "He's sweet and caring and he tells me he misses me."

She raised her eyebrows at me.

"But he has a whole life back there, and none of it involves me. And he seemed to be really excited about what he's had going on these past few days, and I can't help but feel like he's moving on without me," I rambled.

"You really love him, don't you?" she asked softly.

I looked up from where I'd been fiddling with the hem of my dress. "More than I thought was possible," I answered sincerely.

"You know what, Lexie girl, I bet this will all work out, you'll see."

"How do you know?"

"I just know." She tapped the end of my nose. "Now come on, I need a wine."

I looked at her expectantly, waiting for the penny to drop.

"Oh crap, well, I'll have a wine; you'll have to settle for a juice."

I giggled and dabbed at my eyes. "I might just head back to my room."

"Nonsense," she argued, pulling me to my feet. "One drink, honey, and I'll let you go. Trust me; it'll be good for you."

I sighed and let her pull me up, it was useless arguing with this woman, there was a reason she was so good at her job – she always got what she wanted.

"Fine," I grumbled. "But I can't promise I'll be good company."

"Oh, you'll be great." She threw her arm casually around my shoulders. "Come and meet my new hire, he's pretty easy on the eye."

"Penny!" I scolded her. "That's inappropriate, I swear, if you try to set me up on a date..."

She just laughed. "I wouldn't do such a thing... but he is *very* pretty," she insisted.

"Penny..." I warned her as she led me down to the bar that now apparently had a pretty boy running it.

"I'm just pulling your leg." She laughed like the crazy old bat she was.

She dragged me into the Alchemy bar and sat me down on a bar stool, all the while looking around, presumably for the new man she had running the show.

I opened my mouth to tell her to sit down, but she disappeared behind the bar before I had a chance.

I turned, my back to the bar and glanced around. It was busy in here tonight, there were people milling around the bar, the ocean view tables, and there were also several couples dotted around the open space. Some were snuggled up in the booth, one was sitting close at a table, their legs touching underneath.

I miss him.

I felt the tears well in my eyes again.

I need to get out of here.

I felt one of the bar staff rest something on the bar behind me, and I opened my mouth, ready to turn down their request for a drink order. But what I wasn't prepared for, was the goosebumps that covered my body when he spoke.

"What can I get for you, my little song bird?"

"The one thing I know for sure is that feelings are rarely mutual, so when they are, drop everything, forget belongings and expectations, forget the games, the two days between texts, the hard to gets because this is it, this is what the entire world is after and you've stumbled upon it by chance, by accident – so take a deep breath, take a step forward, now run, collide like planets in the system of a dying sun, embrace each other with both arms and let all the rules, the opinions and common sense crash down around you. Because this is love, kid, and it's all yours. Believe me, you're in for one hell of a ride, after all – this is the one thing I know for sure."

- Beau Taplin

32. Colt

I watched as her skin prickled with awareness, all from my words – she recognized my voice immediately, like I knew she would. Hell, I would have known her voice anywhere, in any faraway corner of this earth.

She froze for a moment, as though she didn't really believe it was me, here, on her cruise ship.

She turned in slow motion, the stool swiveling underneath her ass.

The moment she laid eyes on me I saw all the breath leave her lungs. The weight lifting off her shoulders was so evident it nearly knocked me back a step.

"Colt?" she asked as if her eyes and ears might have been deceiving her.

"I got you, babe," I told her softly.

Her eyes welled with tears. "You're here... oh my god, you're here." She reached for me, but I didn't want the barrier between us.

Never taking my eyes off her for one second, I rounded the bar as quickly as I could.

She met me halfway and lunged for me, knowing full well that I'd never let her fall.

"Lexie." I breathed in a sigh of relief as I wrapped my arms tight around her, right where they belonged. My chin rested on the top of her head – she was the exact right height and she fit against me so perfectly; it was as though her body had been designed to match mine... as though she had been made specifically for me.

"I missed you." She sobbed against my chest.

"I know, I'm so sorry, Lex." I attempted to soothe her, running my hands up and down her back. "I'm here now and I'm not leaving unless you tell me to."

"But the ship's left port," She gaped, pulling back suddenly as though she'd only just reached the realization that I was really here, on this ship that she called home. "You're stuck on here for two weeks." She looked like she was going to start crying again.

"I'm not *stuck* anywhere," I reassured her. "And besides, I'll be here a lot longer than that anyway." I gestured to the bar behind us.

Her bloodshot eyes darted back and forth between me and the bar until her brain made the connection.

"You came to work *here*... for me? *You're* the pretty new bar manager?"

I chuckled at the pretty reference. "Everything is for you, Lexie."

"But your life? The club? Your apartment? Oh my god what about Betsy and all the others, who will visit them?" She spoke in such a rush I wasn't entirely sure I'd caught it all.

"Breathe, baby, it's okay, I'll explain everything... and the oldies are fine, I promised I'd write and visit when I could. I even tried to show them how to work Skype, so we'll see how that goes."

She looked up at me, her eyes wide and panicked.

"None of that matters now, Lexie, It's just you and me," I reassured her as I brushed her hair from her face.

She smiled, but shook her head slightly in disagreement at the same time.

I frowned, not understanding.

"Yeah, ah..." She cleared her throat awkwardly. "We ummm... can we talk?" she replied, her expression suddenly more nervous than I'd ever seen her.

What the hell?

Her words were terrifying me, but the smile on her face was soothing. I didn't know what to make of it. My mind raced through the possibilities, but came up empty.

I searched her eyes for answers but she just laughed lightly. "I tried to call you," she scolded me, smacking me lightly on the shoulder.

"I was on a plane," I replied, pulling her close again and nuzzling my face into her shoulder. I couldn't get close enough. "On my way to get my girl."

"We need to talk," she insisted softly.

"Off you go, you two, Mikey has things under control here," Penny called from behind the bar.

I twisted so I could see her, still holding Lexie tight against me. I wondered absently if the woman had mind reading abilities or supersonic hearing.

"Are you sure?" I asked.

She waved her hand dismissively. "Yes, I'm sure," she insisted. "You two have some catching up to do." She winked at me and I realized that she knew exactly what Lexie needed to talk to me about.

I also came to the conclusion that I was probably the worst employee in the history of this cruise ship right now, but since I didn't technically start until tomorrow, I was going to let it slide, just this once.

"Lead the way," I instructed Lexie.

***

Lexie was pacing the small room. Seven steps in one direction, turn, seven steps back.

I'd sat down on the edge of her bed – *our* bed, and was waiting her out, I'd expected her to come right out with it, but apparently she wasn't quite ready to spill her guts just yet.

I didn't care how long she took. The only thing that I needed was in this room right now... I had all the time in the world.

"You okay, baby?" I asked her in amusement.

"Colt! It's not funny," she groaned. She paused momentarily, and then took up her pacing again, walking in the opposite direction this time.

"Is it bad?" I asked her, more serious in my question now. Truthfully, I was starting to get a little worried about what she needed to tell me.

Has she met someone else?

I shoved that thought far from my mind. When it came to Lexie and I, there was, and never would be anyone else.

"No... it's just... I don't know how you'll take it... I..."

I stood up, grabbed her mid step and crouched slightly to look into her beautiful blue eyes. "Lexie..." I soothed. "We can deal with it, whatever it is... just tell me, babe."

She stared right back at me, her eyes swimming with fear.

"I'm... I... We're..." she stuttered, glancing down.

I tipped her chin up so she was looking at me again and gave her a nod to tell me.

"I'm pregnant," she breathed. The words were so quiet I wasn't sure I'd even heard right.

My eyes darted down to her still-flat stomach in disbelief. "You're pregnant?"

She nodded. "We're going to be parents," she answered me with more strength in her voice this time.

"We're having a baby?"

She's carrying my baby?

She nodded, her nerves pouring off her in waves.

Holy shit.

"We're having a baby!" I fist pumped the air before dragging her up into my arms and squeezing her tight.

I'm gonna be a dad.

"You're not mad?" she asked between giggles.

"Mad? Why would I be mad?" I quizzed as I set her down to her feet.

"Because we actively tried to prevent this..." She shrugged sheepishly.

I knew now why she'd been such a mess on the stage. She'd been all alone, trying to deal with some of the most life-changing news that could happen to a person. I wasn't here, and she had no idea how I'd react.

Idiot – she doesn't even know I love her.

I sat down on the bed and tugged her into my lap. "I couldn't be further from mad, baby."

I swept the hair off her face and looked into her eyes. "I owe you an apology."

She shook her head quickly in disagreement. "You don't owe me anything."

"I do," I insisted. "I never should have let you get on that plane alone. I should have come with you, or made you stay with me. We should have figured something better out. I shouldn't have let you go, Lexie."

She opened her mouth to argue but I silenced her with a look. I still had more to say.

"You and I are meant to be together." I looked into her deep blue eyes, hoping that I was showing her exactly how I felt. "Everything is better when I'm with you, Lexie, and I'm sorry it took me so long, and god, I'm so sorry that you felt alone with this news, but I'm here now, and I swear to whatever kind of god you might believe in, I'm not going anywhere."

"You've only known me less than a month," she argued.

"I feel like I've known you a lot longer than that." I ran my thumb over her bottom lip and her eyes closed at the contact. "And I promise, it took me a hell of a lot less time than that to fall in love with you."

Her eyes flicked open. "You're in love with me?" she asked quietly.

I chuckled lightly. Of course I was in love with her. I fell in love with her a lifetime ago.

"Are you not in love with me?" I asked her instead.

She blushed, her cheeks going a beautiful pink color. "I love you more than anything in the world," she confirmed.

I knew she loved me, she may not have said the words aloud, but she told me with her actions, the words she didn't say and the way she looked at me.

I just knew.

Lexie Chase had been head over heels in love with me before she even got on that plane to go home, as I had been with her. But there was nothing quite like hearing those precious words flowing from her mouth.

"I should have told you I loved you," I told her, regret in my voice.

"I should have told you too."

"I'll make it up to you," I promised. "How about I tell you every single day for the rest of forever?"

"Promise?" She smiled.

"Swear on my life."

I'd never made a promise that would be so easy to keep.

I held her tight, breathing in the scent that was home to me now. It didn't matter if we lived in here, or back home, or even on a cruise ship, if Lex was there, I was home.

I tentatively reached a hand out for her belly. It felt stupid, there was nothing showing there yet, but knowing my baby was snuggled up safe in there was a feeling I couldn't even describe.

Lexie smiled at me, so sweetly as I gently caressed her stomach. I could tell she was close to tears.

"When will be we meeting this little peanut?" I asked fondly.

"I don't know." She shrugged. "All I've done is pee on a stick."

"Well at least we'll be able to give the doc a definite date." I chuckled.

"I can't believe we made a baby the first time we had sex," she replied in disbelief. "Who does that?"

"It's my superhuman sperm," I told her with a grin.

She rolled her eyes, and snuggled in closer to me. I could feel her placing soft kisses to my chest.

"Are you okay, babe? I know we didn't plan for this... if you don't want this yet, we can... we can talk about other options," I offered.

Those words burned coming out of my mouth. I didn't want to discuss other options. I wanted this baby. I wanted it with Lexie. We might have been a few years ahead of planning for a child, but we were here now and I wouldn't change it for anything.

She looked up into my eyes. "There is nothing I want more in my life than you and our baby."

Well thank god for that.

***

"I can't believe your brother just turned up like that, what are the chances?" she mused. "And then Penny offering you a job..."

It was meant to be.

"You asked me if I believed in fate, you remember that?"

She nodded and smiled.

"Well you bet your sweet little ass, if I didn't entirely believe in it before, I do now."

She giggled softly.

"But job or not, I was getting on this ship, I even paid for a room as a guarantee."

"How nice of a room?" she asked quickly with an eyebrow raised.

I chuckled deep in my belly, already knowing where this was going. "A damn nice room," I replied. "They only had the most expensive kind left and I was out of options."

"Does it have a balcony?" she asked, her eyes getting more excited by the minute. "And its own bathroom?" She bounced up and down on the spot.

I laughed again; she was just so damn cute. "You bet, baby."

"Holy shit, what are we still doing down here? I love this job, but the sleeping arrangements suck, big time."

I had to agree. No doubt Lexie had one of the better rooms, being the star performer on the ship, but still, it was a dark, five meter by five meter box with not much more than a bed in it.

I picked her bag up and dropped it onto the bed with a thud. "Get your crap together, the high life is waiting, my princess."

"That's when you know for sure somebody loves you. They figure out what you need and they give it to you – without you asking."
- Adriana Trigian

33. Lexie

He came for me.

I couldn't believe Colt had come all the way out here.

For me...

I was still in a complete state of shock, and I wasn't even the one who'd just had the news of impending parenthood dropped on them.

He'd joked, calling me his princess, but that was exactly how I felt when he was around. He treated me like I was his entire world.

Because I am.

It was a surreal feeling, knowing that you were loved. Knowing without a doubt that the person you loved, loved you back. I couldn't explain it. I just found myself looking at him and thinking... that of all of the millions of people in this world, *he* chose *me*. And the best bit was that he looked back at me like he was thinking the same about me.

Colt hadn't been kidding when he said he'd paid for a nice room. The room we'd been living in for the past three days was possibly the nicest room I'd ever seen on this ship. It must have cost him an absolute fortune.

Besides the obvious luxury of a suite, I was incredibly grateful for the privacy of the bathroom. Morning sickness had made itself known to me and I'd been puking my guts out ever since.

I still had no idea why it was referred to as 'morning sickness', because that shit seemed to hit me at *any* time of the day, much to the concern of my very doting boyfriend.

Colt had dragged me to the on-ship doctor yesterday, albeit kicking and screaming. The doctor had managed to get me some anti-nausea medication that was safe for the baby, and I begrudgingly had to admit that it had helped a little. Now I was only throwing up first thing in the morning or if I went too long without food.

Colt was fussing over me like some kind of mother hen, deciding for me that I wasn't fit to perform. I'd tried to argue, but ended up throwing up again.

                    NICOLE S. GOODIN

Needless to say, he won that argument. He had Penny on his side anyway, and there was no arguing with her.

"I'm so glad you're here," I told him for the hundredth time as he rubbed my feet for me. We had the door open onto our balcony and the warm Hawaiian air was breezing through the room.

This was seriously the life. I found myself wishing that I was just here for a holiday and not for my job. That feeling was an entirely foreign one to me. I *loved* my job. I'd worked damn hard to land it, and I had no intentions of leaving.

Or did I?

"I forgot to tell you." Colt suddenly flicked his eyes up to mine. "Mitch is having a baby with his new fiancée." His eyes were glowing and I could tell he was incredibly excited about this news.

"You're going to be a daddy *and* an uncle." I beamed at him.

"God, I love it when you say that," he told me, a huge smile gracing his perfect face.

"How'd you manage to forget to tell me that?" I frowned at him, going from thinking he was cute, to a tad annoying... all in a matter of seconds.

Damn hormones.

He laughed at me and shrugged sheepishly. "I think I got a bit distracted by the 'we're having a baby' news and then the puking started and it's been a bit crazy ever since."

"Touché... tell me now," I encouraged.

So he did. I learned all about what had brought his brother home from the military and how he'd managed to score himself a beautiful wife-to-be.

"We'll be having our babies only a few months apart," I mused.

We'd gotten out a calendar and attempted to figure out when this baby was going to be entering the world – all going to plan. We'd worked it out that we'd be having a July baby, since we were only a few weeks along right now. Sophia and Mitch were due in late March.

"It's going to be so cool for them growing up as cousins so close in age." I smiled as I thought about it. I always hoped I'd have children with someone who had siblings. Being an only child, my children wouldn't get any cousins from my side of the family, and I was ecstatic that this baby would have a partner in crime.

"Yeah." Colt smiled back at me, but it didn't reach his eyes.

"What's wrong?" I asked quickly. I was so in tune with this man, he couldn't get anything by me anymore.

"Nothing." He shook his head and smiled, and this time it was dazzling. "Absolutely nothing is wrong with my life right now, I've got everything I need right here." He squeezed my hand and I knew he was being totally truthful.

"But?" I prompted. I knew him well enough by now to know that there was still something small bothering him.

He sighed. "It just sucks that I won't be a *present* uncle, ya know? That our kids won't actually grow up together... I guess I just imagined that Harrison, Mitch and me would always be around for each other and our kids, just like we were when we were growing up. We always had each other."

For some reason that explanation made tears spring to my eyes. I could understand why that was important to him. Hell, in just the few seconds since he'd mentioned it, it had become important to me too.

"Do you think..." I asked hesitantly. "That maybe... we should talk about moving back to your home before the baby comes?"

His eyes shot up from where he'd started rubbing my feet again.

"You'd consider that?" he asked, his expression one of total awe.

I bit down on my bottom lip and nodded my head shyly. "Yeah, I would."

His jaw fell lax.

"I think raising a baby surrounded by family and friends is the perfect way to do it."

He smiled a smile that was so breathtaking, and I knew he couldn't find the words to say what he wanted to say.

I knew right then that we would be moving. He looked so overjoyed at just the idea of it.

How could I say no?

Why would I want to?

He was here. He'd uprooted his entire life to come here for me, the least I could do was offer the same in return.

His eyes darkened and smoldered as he leaned over in almost slow motion and reached for his phone.

"What are you doing?" I asked, my voice husky from the look in his eyes.

"I'm checking Google to see if we can have sex while you're pregnant."

I threw my head back and laughed. "Of course we can, babe."

"I want to make sure," he insisted as he tapped away on his phone. It struck me right then and there that Colt was totally going to be one of those adorable fathers-to-be that read all of the pregnancy books, and one who was going to be there through every single stage of this thing with a smile on his face.

I can't wait.

"It's fine, babe, trust me." I took the phone from his hand and sat it back down on the small table.

He tugged on my hand and I moved to sit in his lap.

"How do you know? I already feel like I'm so far behind," he asked as he ran the tip of his nose up and down the side of my neck.

It would have been cool to say that I knew even one single thing about being pregnant, but I didn't, other than the fact that it took nine months, I was totally clueless.

"I might have asked the doctor when you left the room." I giggled.

"Fiend." He chuckled as he placed a kiss on the skin just below my ear.

I shuddered. It had been far too long since we'd been together like this.

"I've missed you," I moaned as he nibbled on the lobe of my ear.

***

I couldn't remember ever feeling this sated. Colt had worshipped every single inch of my body from top to bottom. It had been the first time he'd touched me intimately since he'd arrived here and I didn't know why we'd waited so long.

Probably all the spewing...

He had been so unbelievably cautious, but I wasn't complaining. He'd handled me like I was made of precious glass, and I guess to him, I was. I was carrying his child and I knew exactly how much that meant to him.

My pulse sped up as I thought about how he'd just pleasured me with the magic skills of his tongue.

That man...

"That was incredible." I sighed. "We could just stay here all day and do nothing but that and I'd be a happy woman." I giggled.

Colt pushed up on his elbow to look at me. "That's what I love the most about you," he told me, pure adoration in his eyes.

"What?" I whispered, already blushing from the compliment that I knew was coming.

"You're just so real, Lexie. You're so present in every moment that we spend together and I know, just by looking at you, that someone could swoop in and offer you everything in the world, and you'd still rather be right here with me."

"I would," I promised. "I'll always choose you."

"I know," he replied simply. "And I don't know how on earth I managed to get you, but I'm keeping you forever. You're kind and gentle, and you've got the most amazing blue eyes I've ever seen in my entire life. You're funny and sassy, and you're a little bit kooky sometimes... and I love that about you – I love everything about you."

Tears welled in my eyes – my hormones were all over the place at the moment.

"I love you, Lexie, there's nothing I wouldn't do for you and our beautiful little munchkin."

Colt was one hundred percent convinced we were having a girl. He 'had a feeling'. I had no feeling either way, not yet anyway, so for now I was letting him have it.

"Do you wanna know what I love the most about you?" I asked him softly as I traced the curve of his bicep with my fingertips.

"Tell me," he mumbled. His eyes were fixed on the path my fingers were travelling.

"I love that you're not afraid to just be you, other people's opinions be damned. I love that you don't shy away from being vulnerable... you're not scared to put yourself out there and risk getting hurt."

I leaned forward and kissed his toned arm.

"You're not one of those guys who puts on an act and hides behind some type of false bravado instead of just telling a person how they feel. I love that you're the kind of man who stops in the street to pet a dog... the kind who spends time in a retirement village to brighten up the lives of a group of old people. I love that you're just *you*. You don't want to be anything other than yourself."

I glanced back at him.

He was watching me closely and his eyes were blazing with a million unsaid feelings.

Love, possession, desire, need, respect...
There was no end to this... there was no end to us.

"I'll never finish falling in love with you."
- Nicole Williams

Epilogue

Colt
Three months later.

"Are you ready for this?" Lex asked me with a grin. She was so relaxed about this whole thing, and I was glad, hell, I was thrilled. It was the best feeling in the world to see that she was as happy about sharing this news as I was.

"They're gonna judge us so hard, you know that right? This timing is not socially acceptable," I joked.

"I never liked social constraints anyway," she drawled.

"You like your friends," I pointed out.

"And *our* friends will be happy for us," she insisted.

I knew she was right, everyone here knew how much we loved each other – they were going to be thrilled for us, social standards be damned.

She pinched my ass as I opened the door to the restaurant where we were meeting my brothers with Quinn and Sophia, and Ellerslie and Lawson for dinner, and I laughed. Some women got put off having sex when they were pregnant, but not my Lexie. She wanted it twenty-four-seven, and I was more than happy to oblige. I'd even joked about keeping her pregnant for the next ten years if she was always going to be this eager for a piece of me.

I was excited, but nervous to be meeting up with everyone tonight. They all thought we just wanted to catch up before we went back for our next cruise, but we had a much bigger announcement in mind for tonight. We'd flown in only earlier today and they were under the impression that we were heading back tomorrow.

We weren't.

I glanced down at the oversized coat that Lexie was wearing. The minute she took that off, the cat would be out of the bag anyway.

194

I still had to pinch myself, every single day that I was here with her. I was so happy sometimes I thought it must have been a dream that I was going to wake up from at any second.

I knew it wasn't everyone's thing, but Lexie and I were both perfectly content spending every moment we could together. In a way, that trait had always been a part of me; I knew I'd always been a little clingy. I'd spent so much time trying to tone down that part of myself for the wrong women, rather than looking for the woman who wanted the same things I did.

Lexie was undoubtedly that woman.

The two of us were like thunder and lightning. One didn't exist without the other.

She'd confessed to missing me when she had to leave me to go and sing for an hour, or take her music classes. When I worked, and she didn't, she was always in her spot, down the end of the bar, either drinking an orange juice, reading a book, writing in the pregnancy planner I'd brought her, or making easy conversation with the staff or patrons.

Work had never felt so easy.

It was going to be strange, moving back here and not working together anymore, but I had a feeling that Lex would be taking up a permanent spot at the end of whatever bar I worked.

***

"We're moving back here," Lexie blurted out when she was finally able to get a moment of silence from the chattering of the group.

"What?"

"Oh my god, what?"

"That is so cool!"

"Seriously, bro?"

The replies fired rapidly at us.

Lexie beamed up at me. She was so excited to make this move. Obviously, from their responses, our friends and family were excited too, and we hadn't even got to the biggest news of all yet.

Lexie grinned at Quinn and El before squeezing my hand under the table, and I knew she was about to drop the bombshell. "I'm so excited!" she squeaked. "We just decided that we'd rather raise a baby here than back home... and so here we are."

I smirked into my glass, waiting for the penny to drop.

The girls were so excited about the fact that they'd be having Lex here with them; they still hadn't stopped to think about what she'd just revealed.

Harrison was the first to realize. His jaw went slack and his eyes flashed over to meet mine.

"Are you... is she?" he stuttered, pointing at Lexie.

I nodded, a massive grin on my face. I slung my arm around Lex, pulling her close, at the same moment that Quinn figured it out.

"Holy shit, are you pregnant?" she yelled, causing half the restaurant to stop what they were doing and look our way.

Lexie giggled and nodded.

"You're having a baby?" El shrieked, looking back and forth between the two of us.

"We're having a baby!" I announced loudly, just in case anyone in the whole place had missed the memo.

I couldn't make out many sentences or words from the few minutes that followed, but if the smiles, hugs, tears and bump-rubbing were anything to go by, everyone was incredibly happy for us.

Mitch sidled up next to me and bumped his shoulder into mine. "Who would have thought you and I would be contributing to the population, huh, little bro?"

"Another five or so months, man, I can't wait." I glanced sideways at him and grinned.

The fact that my baby would get to grow up alongside his or her cousin and eventually *cousins* here, had played a big part in us making the move back out here. I wasn't close with my parents so I didn't really factor them into the equation... Lexie's Mom and her husband lived in a fair way away, and her Dad and his wife weren't any closer, so it didn't make a lot of difference to either of their travel time for visits.

"So you fell in love for real this time, huh?" he taunted me, his own love-filled eyes on his fiancée.

I chuckled. Mitch might have given me a hard time in the past for believing that I'd been in love so often, but he knew that this time was different for me.

I looked at Lex and knew that I'd fallen in love for the first and last time.

"I fell in crazy, stupid, life-changing love, man."

"That's the best way to do it." He tipped his chin in Sophia's direction. "I didn't know what hit me when I met Soph... most days I still don't know how I got so lucky."

I knew exactly what he meant. I still woke up every day and had to check next to me to make sure she was there... that I hadn't dreamed the whole thing up.

"You got room at that club for one more?" I nudged his arm with my elbow.

He looked at me out the corner of his eye, his brow raised. "You for real?"

I nodded.

"Thank god, the place is going to shit without you."

I chuckled. I knew he was joking, but it was a nice feeling to be welcomed back with open arms.

It was so good to be back. I hadn't realized how much I would miss the place once I was gone.

I'm so happy we're moving.

I already knew that our decision to move here was the right choice. We'd gone back and forth, written pro and cons lists... we didn't take the decision lightly. Penny had ended up being the real deciding factor. Lexie had been so nervous to tell her that we were considering making the move back. She was convinced that Penny would be disappointed, even hurt that we wanted to move away.

That couldn't have been further from the truth.

Penny had been upset, sure, but only that she wouldn't be able to squish the baby's cheeks whenever she wanted – her words, not mine. There had been some tears, but she was so happy for us, and agreed that we were making the right decision, as long as we agreed to come back and visit at least once a year.

She'd even surprised us both by pulling some strings job wise. We had both been offered jobs upon a sister ship that departed from the local port. It was an incredible opportunity, like someone had just picked up our lives and transferred them to here.

Surprisingly though, Lexie had declined her offer, and in turn so had I. She didn't want to be raising a baby on a ship, and she'd finally realized that her voice was worthy of being in a recording studio – she'd had numerous contract offers already and we were working through some of the terms, together. I intended to come back to the club and work alongside my brother to make 'The L' even better than ever.

There wasn't anything more I could ask for.

I would have a job that I enjoyed, a beautiful woman that I intended to spend every minute of forever with, a baby that I already loved more than my own life growing in her belly, and family and friends surrounding me that I wouldn't change for the world. Even the little cottage we'd bought on the outskirts of town was perfect for us.

Just like I imagined.

I wouldn't change a damn thing.

I smiled as I watched Lexie, Quinn on one side of her, and El on the other, each of them with a hand on her cute little bump. She was the most precious thing in the world to me – she was *everything*, and she was mine.

God, she's beautiful.

When I looked at her smile, her eyes, heard her giggle or watched her speak, I knew that I was going to spend the rest of my life doing exactly that.

Nobody had more in this moment than I did.

***

Another five or so months later

I was right... it was a girl – a perfect little girl.

Just like her momma.

Other Titles

Love like Yours Series

Rushed – Book 1
Pierced – Book 2
Hunted – Book 3
Chased – Book 4

Rock Games Novels

Paper, Scissors, Rock: Vol. 1
Hide and Seek: Vol. 2

The Heart Duet

My Heart Needs
My Heart Wants

Acknowledgements

I was never too sure if I'd get as far as book four, I half expected book one to be a giant failure and that I'd slink away into the shadows with my tail between my legs.

I couldn't be happier that that's not the case.

I want to thank all of the friends I've made in the book world in the past year. All the tips and advice are so appreciated. There's nothing quite like having people to bounce ideas off, and it's pretty cool to have people to talk to when our characters decide to do all kinds of crazy stuff.

Thanks for not thinking I'm going crazy with all these voices in my head – or for at least accepting that you're just as crazy as I am!

Thanks to everyone who has read my books, the support means so much to me and I hope you enjoyed Lexie and Colt's story. A lot of readers had a soft spot for Colt after Hunted, and I hope that you're all satisfied with the happily ever after he's found with sweet little Lexie.

Thank you again!

About the Author

NICOLE S. GOODIN is a romance author and mother of two from Taranaki in the North Island of New Zealand.

Mid 2015, she started to write about a group of characters who wouldn't get out of her head. Her first book, Rushed, was published in mid 2016, then Pierced, late 2016, Hunted, early 2017, and Chased, mid 2017.

Nicole enjoys long walks on the beach, pillow fights and braiding her friends' hair. She dislikes clichés, talking about herself in the third person, and people who don't understand her sense of humor.

Please feel free to contact her either via her website, email, Instagram, Twitter or on her Facebook page, she would love to hear your feedback. If you're feeling really game, you can even sign up for her newsletter.